T0129133

SABOTAGE

BRITTANY HOWARD

authorHOUSE®

AuthorHouse™
1663 Liberty Drive
Bloomington, IN 47403
www.authorhouse.com
Phone: 1 (800) 839-8640

Published by AuthorHouse 05/09/2017

ISBN: 978-1-5246-9169-1 (sc)
ISBN: 978-1-5246-9168-4 (e)

Library of Congress Control Number: 2017907341

Print information available on the last page.

Any people depicted in stock imagery provided by Thinkstock are models, and such images are being used for illustrative purposes only. Certain stock imagery © Thinkstock.

This book is printed on acid-free paper.

ACKNOWLEDGMENTS

I just want to acknowledge that this short novel is a work of fiction. Any character names I used to write this book isn't to involve or reference no real people in my life past or present. Not even myself, I wanted to give the readers a sense of my imagination and wicked thoughts. Also, to share with them that anything you put your mind to you can achieve. With focus preparation and dedication, you can accomplish anything. Keep god first, and have faith in everything you do.

First, I want to thank god for giving me the vision to write this book. I thank him for his love, grace and the strength he gives me to have goals and execute them. All praise and glory goes to him.

Next, I would like to thank my mom for her everyday love and support. Without her I wouldn't be where or who I am today. The person I'm becoming comes from the love and motivation she gives me. When times are hard or when I'm feeling down I can never hide it, she's right there. For that, I'm very grateful. You're the best mom ever!!!

I also want to thank my mentor Sherelle Hogan for her everyday motivation. She made sure I stayed on my P's and Q's when it came to this book. She makes sure I'm in great spirits, productive and positive every morning. Thank you so much for being a true friend.

To my family and friends, I thank you all for being so true to me. You guys bring out the best in every part of me. My life is filled with nothing but pure joy and laughter on an everyday basis. I couldn't imagine another family or group of friends to have. I love you all soooo much!

I want to thank my Noble Team for inspiring me to chase my dreams, and achieve every goal I set out for myself. You women make it all possible for me, because you believe in me. For that I am very thankful.

Also, Special thanks to photographer Marty Watson for an awesome photo cover.

SABOTAGE

Written by: Brittany Howard

Okay now let's be for real who wants to work a nine to five their whole life, letting a white man boss them around slaving in a hot ass factory while a bunch of retired bachelors look at your ass. I tried that, that lifestyle just wasn't for me. I rather take risks and get it the fast way. Finessing dudes at twenty-three may sound a bit too much but face it, school wasn't for me. I tried it for two years straight, living in Ohio was hell. From my country ass roommate to my boring ass professors teaching things he barely even knew. I used to sit in class confused, I could barely pronounce the words. I had to find an easier way out. I thought stripper but I knew if I decided to go down that road I wouldn't be considered that bitch. I would've been another slut chasing all the drug dealers and scammers that walked into the bar. So... I decided to be the good girl and the bad girl. I knew I needed something to cover up my filthy lifestyle. I had to come up with something to throw them off. I considered myself a "Business woman" for the bitches that wanted to know my business so bad. Saying that would've been most clever so I ran with that. I had to think of something quick, for the simple fact the money was coming too fast and I needed something to cover me. I needed the world to know my money was legal and clean and if they ever found out I was tricking for cash my reputation would be ruined. So, let's be real what's a girl to do when her needs need to be fulfilled. When her rents due. When she's hungry and has nothing to eat. When she can't depend on family for shit, she had to hustle and even though tricking sound a bit degrading. Fuck it, I had to do what I had to do.

CHAPTER 1

Aw Man, I hope I can make this flight. I knew I should've gone with my first mind and just stayed home last night. But hell, it was my last night in Ohio and I was going to miss my best friends Drew and Simone. We've been inseparable since 7th grade. It was such a bitter sweet feeling to say goodbye to them for the last time, running through the airport with two suitcases and a small tote that had a broken strap. I was so nervous. Knowing I couldn't have missed this flight or this oppor-tunity I had waiting for me, I had to run full speed. For the simple fact, I didn't have an extra five hundred dollars to rebook my flight and with me being a poor freshman in college I was too cheap to purchase trip protection. All I knew was I didn't want to stay living in a small dorm room at a community college for another three years. Well worst, after vh1 new hit show called me back for auditions I cursed out my financial advisor saying I didn't need them and how happy I was to leave that dirty bird nest of a school. I mean I always got in trouble for my mouth. My mouth was slicker than worm sperm. If I would have missed the flight I would've been homeless because wasn't no way in hell I was moving back to Ohio.

Finally making it to the gate, I showed the flight attendant my boarding pass. I hope I get a window seat & I hope I don't end up sitting next to an old ass man that loves talking about his 1963 childhood with strangers. I'd rather sit next to the lady with the crying baby that whines the whole flight. I will even settle for a nice calm lady that likes to read so she keeps the reading light on and the air conditioner knob turned toward the both of us, anything but talking bob. As the plane took off Viola put her headphones in and closed her eyes.

Waking up just in time for landing Viola opened her window and seen complete sunshine. Welcome to Springfield Illinois, its 103 degrees all sunny today. Thanks for flying spirit hope you guys enjoy your visit until we see you again.

103 degrees, oh hell naw. I have on a Victoria secret jogging suit and Nikes. I guess I should have checked the weather beforehand. Viola stepped off the plane walking through the huge airport looking for baggage claim. She spotted a girl she went to school with back in 9th grade. Mona is that you. Viola yelled out. Viola!! Heyyy girl what are you doing here. I'm surprised you remembered me Mona said running towards Viola. Last time I seen you, you and drew showed the whole class a video of me falling at that skating party we had that one year. I was so embarrassed. I remem-bered that day like yesterday you guys teased me the whole year, I never wanted to come back to Mr. Johnson's class for the rest of that semester. Of course, I remember you and that, Viola stared at her uncomfortable and embarrassed, but I mean you wasn't my friend you

were close with my best friend Simone, trying to change the subject. How is she? Mona asked. She's great she just lost her dad so that's been rough but she's still crazy ass Simone. Take my number and maybe we can link up soon. I live here now, so I'm always around. Mona concluded. Oh, okay that's cool. I'm here for auditions, but I plan on never moving back home so I guess I can call this home.

Viola splitted ways with Mona, flagging a taxi down' not knowing where to go. All she knew was that she had auditions the next day at 3pm and it was to come at your own expenses. I'm sure they didn't think anyone would fly out for some auditions they may not make but Viola was so eager and determined that she had to do what she had to do. With only four hundred dollars left in her wallet. She seen a motel 6 with a sign so bold in the sky saying specials $54 bucks a night. Ordering the cab driver to turn into the first driveway, she grabbed her bags and made her way into the motel.

Wow, this is worse than my dorm room. Staring at herself in the mirror, I have to kill these auditions tomorrow. I hope it's simple. I don't know what I'm getting my-self into or what they want me to say or do but what I do know if all was to fail, the lord won't let me down. I stepped out on faith so I know he will bless me. Laying her outfit out neatly on the bed, Viola laid down to rest.

The next morning Viola was waking up by a Mexican lady yelling room service. Room service, I wouldn't eat a rice Krispy treat from this place. No thank you, I'm about to leave now, Yelling back at the house keeper. Viola showered slipped on her clothes and headed down stairs to flag a cab.

After auditions Viola found the nearest restaurant her stomach was growling like a hibernating bear, regretting the fact she turned down the Breakfast at the motel ear-lier. She seen a close Wendy's in which that was the only drive thru place she could relate to so she stopped there to smash.

The lady said she will be calling me a bit later, maybe I can get in touch with Mona and have her show me around. I mean I never hung with her in high school she was always dorky as shit to me. But hell, I didn't have a clue to how I was going to get around this big ass city and I knew I wasn't about to keep breaking twenty after twenty on these cab rides. If they don't call me back with good news I'm ruined. Dialing Mona, there was no answer. Great! I guess I'll go to the mall and window shop until I get the call from vh1. The skits were easy, even though I stumbled a few times with my fake ass Naomi Campbell walk. They had me posing dancing and talking all at once. I was dizzy as hell. I was never great at multitasking. But that was my only chance. I had to make it do what it do.

As Viola walked the mall, she felt her phone vibrating at the bottom of her purse. Fidgeting through her Michael kors bags she had almost missed the most Important call. Tina is her name, she said she will only call once and she will not leave a voicemail.

Hello. hello is this Viola? Yes, this is Viola. Hi, I'm co director for the new television series you just auditioned for. I just wanted to let you know that your job was unique and tasteful, but we decided to go with a more experience and skilled candidate. Thank you for auditioning with us. And good luck to you on your future endeavors. Click.

Viola stared at the phone so mortified and loss of words. Stuck and confused on what she was going to do with her life. I can't believe he called me to tell me bad news. He could've saved himself the trouble and that pointless ass phone call. Throwing her phone back into her purse, taking a last sip of her strawberry lemonade she had been babysitting for the longest. As she sat down by a fountain filled with change. What's luck? She said digging into her purse to find a quarter, she made a wish and tossed it into the fountain.

What am I going to do now? I don't have enough funds to get back home, I don't know anyone from here but Mona and she's not answering. I guess I'll call my mom in the morning and have her send for me.

Viola thought to herself as she pressed 1 on the elevator.

The next morning Mona had returned Viola call. She said she would be in route in another 30 minutes, plenty of time for me to get myself together. Viola knew at this point it was to go hard or go home. She knew if she finessed Mona into feeling sorry for her she would get in good and have somewhere to lay her head for a couple of days. Mona was always gullible so it was easy to tell a sob story, and at this point I didn't care if she lived in someone's basement, I needed free shelter.

Mona arrived at the motel as Viola struggled putting all her luggage in the trunk. Going straight into acting mode with a devastating look Mona asked what was wrong?

Girl, just another day of being Viola. Always trying to do things her way and things never go as plan. I didn't get the part for the TV series. So now I'm trying to figure out my next move. Viola said to Mona. Girl my aunt has a shelter for women all you have to do is go sign up and they will give u a bed and a free meal every morning. I mean that's not a lot. I know you're used to

Nice things but it'll work for now until you get on your feet. Mona gave Viola a flyer and address to the shelter as she showed her the city.

At that point, Viola knew she couldn't finesse her into staying with her but from the looks of her backseat she didn't have a place to stay herself. She had underwear and pumps all over the place.

As they visited the north south and east side of Springfield's they were wore out. Viola was lowkey tired of seeing Mona's face so she just asked if she could drop her off at the nearest motel and she would take it from there. It was a nice night, Viola heard some guys at this bar and grill say something about Pablo's on a Thursday night. I heard that hoe be jamming. As Viola showered and got dressed for the night, she had to remember who she was and where she came from. Wasn't know show going to stop her from living out her dreams. She knew she had to get super fine and put on her Saturdays best night clothes to meet some potential ballers.

As she arrived at Pablo's, her eyes couldn't believe what they were seeing. She had never seen so many foreign cars and diversity of people in her life. Back at home, the whites hung with the whites, the blacks with the blacks and the Asians with the Asians.

Strutting into the club entrance waving her identification at the bouncer who obvi-ously takes his job super serious, he had eyed down the girl in front of me license for the longest. In the back of my mind I wanted to just scream "let her go in already!"

Viola sat by the bar and pretended to order drinks, acting as if she didn't know what to drink. She just didn't want to spend another dime on anything. Luckily the club was free before 11 o'clock. As a light skinned man approached her and offered to buy her a drink. He kindly introduced himself and made conversation. Drink after drink Viola was soon intoxicated and had to go look for a cab. Her phone had no percentage and she was completely wasted. The guy whose name she didn't remem-ber asked to take her home. She was so drunk she didn't even care if she slept in the club. She just wanted to lay down. The next morning Viola woke up laying next to the stranger whom she forgot she met the night before, handing her a wash cloth and tooth brush. Its Tim by the way. Excuse me Viola said. My name is Tim Did we have sex? yes we did. I wasn't about to ask you that. Viola replied. Well you were drunk and I didn't want to make it seem like I raped you so I wanted to remind you. Here's five hundred dollars I called you an uber to take you wherever you wanted to go. Fixing his tie lacing up his black patent leather ferrogamas, she stared at him for a hot second so confused. She didn't want to ask any more questions so she grabbed the money and ran to the bathroom to shower. His house is Immaculate, looking out the window of a luxe condominium everything looked like dots from far up he had to live on the 40th floor.

Uber came just in time Viola got out the shower she was too embarrassed to look at him for the simple fact she felt like a jump off and had a one night stand for the first time. What a slut she said to herself as she closed the door and headed to the elevator.

Take me to the most expensive hotel, she ordered the uber driver to drive her down-town Springfield's. Viola felt rich after he had given her that money. She was up eight hundred fifty-six dollars and was kind of happy about it. I mean that's not a lot of money but it's more than what I started with. I can catch me a flight up out this bitch. Or I can use what I got to get what I want. Here it is Friday night, and I don't even remember what happened last night. If I could get drunk every night like that and have sex with men for a few bucks. I will soon be living comfortable and no one has to know. I mean no one knows me anyway so that makes everything better. Viola pulled up to fantasy stay hotel where they greeted her and the uber driver before she could even get out the car. She knew this place had to be upscale and every bit of 6 stars. She had to plan her operation patiently and smart so that she wouldn't get busted for selling pussy on the streets. She had to make sure she only fucked with top men so they wouldn't be petty about giving her the amount she asked for. She had to make sure her clothes matched her standards, so she took a cab back to the mall and spent two hundred dollars in forever21. Once she got back to the hotel in which she didn't get a room, on the count of they were five hundred bucks a night. She went to the girl's rest room to powder up and slip on her sexiest outfit.

A month later …

CHAPTER 2

UMM. What's this? I told you fifteen hundred. I know but I don't have any loose bills on me. Well give me what you have, this wasn't the agreement! Fifteen hundred and I'll get wet for you. Viola said in a loud tone. Look man take this money and get up out my crib. I don't even know why I let your trick ass taste this. Taste what? Be glad I put my mouth on it, small cock ass nigga. Snatching the money with so much aggravation and storming out the door of a four thousand square feet mansion, Viola jumped in her Mercedes bens she had purchased a week ago and drove off. Pulling up to her condominium she had also paid for a couple of weeks ago, so tired and exhausted! Viola poured herself a glass of sweet red wine and laid across a leather plush sofa, scooting her toes through her animal print pillows. I can't keep living like this, selling my soul to these rappers, drug dealers and athletes. Hell, the money is good. My bills are paid on time. No car note, no rent, who's really fucking with me. Viola thought to herself,. I'm the new bitch in town and I'm only 23! Taking another sip of her wine. Who would of guess a month ago I was down on my luck with my last four hundred dollars. I had no clue what I was going to do. But look at me now I made it happen in one month. Got me a crib, I drive the nicest car that's out on the streets right now and I'm just that bitch!

Viola turned on her favorite soul music station. I can play their music all day every day. It puts me in a good mood every night, she said as she bopped her head to every beat. Her. cell phone started to ring the minute she got into her sexy mood. THIS BETTER NOT BE SIMONE! Digging through her red Chanel bag looking for her phone. RING, RING!!! I'm coming, yelling at the purse still trying to find the phone. Hello, hey bitch you landed yet.

Viola eyes had opened wide, forgetting she had an 8:45 flight. Shit!!! yelling through the phone. I forgot my flight was today! I been so busy and exhausted I missed it. Girl you need to really lay off drinking, it's fucking with your brain cells. Whatever I'll call you back. Viola hung up the phone throwing it back into her purse. How did I forget I had a flight? She talked to herself for a while,. What am I doing??? Ring-Ring, this better not be Simone again, searching through her bag the number read unknown. Hello!! Is this the lovely Viola? Who is this? She stared surprised, knowing that nobody knew her real name especially any one from Springfield. This Niko, you met me in club prime the other night. Club prime? Niko? Well why are you calling me unknown and how do you know my name is Viola. You told me Damn, you weren't that drunk was you? Viola sat quietly on the phone thinking, "damn Simone was right, I got to stop drinking"! Well what's up, what brings you across my number and again why are you calling me unknown. I thought about what you told me the other night and my dick got hard. I called you unknown because my wife be checking my phone. WIFE! Yes, wife Niko repeated. So, what was it I said to you the other night Mr. Niko not even caring about the fact he just mentioned he had a wife. You told me you knew a lot of tricks and would take care of me if I talked the right numbers. SO... so I'm talking one thousand cash. Thousand cash. "Viola negotiated it to herself, okay a thousand cash is cool. Where do you want me to meet you? 702 Broadway avenue at 11 o'clock tonight. Broadway Ave! That's an hour away from where I'm at, too far! You have to meet me somewhere closer. Meet me downtown at the fantasy stay. I can't meet you there my girl sister work there, and what's that supposed to mean? Viola interrupted him,, who's going to notice you walking into a hotel room downtown at 11 o'clock at night?

Everybody will notice me. Who else has a light blue Bentley with tinted windows in the city? Nobody but Niko. Well look I really don't have time for your shenanigans, I'm about my money. I can careless if you catch an Uber, So I'll see you at 11 o'clock! CLICK! Viola hung up her phone and threw it on the kitchen counter. Run-ning her some hot bath water in her oval shaped marble tub, she lit candles through-out the bathroom, turned on kemistry; dropped her towel, sat in the tub and just re-laxed!

An hour later Viola got into her car, counting all her money she had made that week, stashing it into a secret compartment in the backseat.

Speaking into her navigation "fantasy stay" fantasy stay 15 miles (turn right onto i93)

Pulling up in valet Niko sent Viola a text "room 104"

Walking through the luxury hallways of fantasy stay with a long alexander McQueen trench coat, 6in heels, long Brazilian brown hair and red lip stick. Every bell boy stared amazingly as if they seen an angel. Only if they knew what was up under that trench. Absolutely nothing.

After a couple of hours of seducing and tricking. Viola counted her money making sure it was all there. Jumping back into her car, she made sure she kept a low profile and soon sped off. The next morning Viola was awakening by sunlight and her alarm clock going off which read 9 am. She threw her silk Gucci robe around her body, went to the kitchen brewed her some coffee, toasted a bagel, and stepped out on the balcony. She sat her coffee cup on a stand and made her way to the bathroom to shower. Moments later Viola heard a light knock at the door, she slipped her robe back on, peeked through her peep hole, and seen it was Niko. "how do this nigga know where I live"? I know he didn't follow me home. Looking terribly nervous, who is it? Viola whispered. Its Niko! Niko?? what brings you here, how you know where I stay, what u want? Calm down, I'm not stalking you. You left your license in the room, I was kindly returning it. I would've left it but the pussy was great. Trust me I'm no stalker. Can I come in? Viola thought to herself. "Why not, he might want to give me more money for a quickie (giggling) slowly opening the door, peeking into Nikos eyes trying to make sure he wasn't on any shady shit. She opened the door. So, what's up! Thanks for caring enough to bring my Id back that was nice of you. I appreciate it! No problem, Niko nodded. So, what's going on starring directly into her eyes. Viola took a step back, nothing! I was about to get ready for a meeting. A meeting for what, Niko asked. If I told you I would have to kill you, really? No not really but I rather not tell you. But I must get dress! You're kicking me out in so many words. I'll give you a call a bit later, maybe we can finish where we left off, Niko concluded.

Don't you have a wife! Exactly why I'm not married, you guys know nothing about loyalty, Niko lowered his head in disbelief. My wife has cancer. It's hard seeing her like that. I cheat to get my mind off being bitter, "look at me" I'm almost a millionaire, I can have any girl I want. You think I want to be in the house de-pressed all day. I rather get out and enjoy myself. You're sick. Even though Viola whole mentality was get money, forget niggas, she kind of felt some type of way about this certain situation. It wasn't right! Hell, if I was married I'd be mortified just the thought of my husband having several affairs on me while I'm sick. Viola thought to herself "... I'll give you a call later (slamming the door)

Changing her profile into a more sophisticated lady oriented Image. You would have never guessed Viola got down the way she did. She went from Marilyn Monroe to Mrs. Obama in just twenty minutes. VIOLA had volunteered at a youth shelter called saving our girls youth to help girls in need. Without Viola being a hypocrite she had to keep her personal life confidential. I mean no one not even Simone (her bf that is) knew what she did behind closed doors. Viola had all the girls wanting to be just like her. They admired her beauty and aspiration. Some of the girls really looked at her as their role model. "Knowing that" Viola knew she couldn't let her secret get open to the public. Her life would be ruined.

Ladies today we will be spring cleaning in other words getting rid of all things with no matter it could be your old clothes, friendships, relationships, or anything that stops you from becoming a better person, anything with no value, anything that doesn't show Improvement. We will all be great and remembered as women with a plan. Remember ladies, we can't be perfect in the private eye, but in a public atmosphere also. Viola stopped and thought to herself "not just a private eye, but in a public atmosphere" I'm not abiding by my own damn rules. I'll see you ladies next week, same time. Viola had to meet her girlfriends for lunch in an hour knowing she would've been late if she went back home to change out of those hot clothes she just stayed nearby and kept on her upscale outfit.

Sitting by the 5star sushi bar waiting on Elizabeth and Miya to pull up, a tall dark handsome man approached her. "excuse me miss, I couldn't help but notice your long brown hair, may I talk to you? Viola was so amazed at the way he looked she went into a daze not even acknowledging him with a reply. All she could see was handsomeness and a white clean smile. How are you? I'm Viola what's yours? I'm Trey Furgerson I'm standing their waiting on valet to pull my car around and you stood out. I couldn't let you pass me by without getting your number or at least trying, may you walk with me. Well, I was waiting on my friends to arrive but its looks like they are going to be late, so I would love too.

Are you from here, Trey asked! No, I'm from Ohio I just moved here three months ago I'm still trying to get adjusted to the city. I haven't even got a chance to view the city that much with work. What do you do? If you don't mind me asking, Viola had a suspicious look on her face knowing that she couldn't tell him what she did. She decided to talk about her volunteer group instead. That's great, I'm glad to see women trying to make change in today's society. That's just the kind of woman I want in my life. So, what do you do? Mr. Furgerson, well I'm 6'5 I got on Jordan's and basketball shorts. What you think I do? Are you a gym teacher? Viola joked, Trey laughed' I love your spirit I play for the Springfield's hawks. Viola eyes widen, even though she almost already had a clue. Seeing the black rolls Royce pulling up to the front of valet service. It was either that or a drug dealer, shit, I like both.

So can I call you or... hesitating to continue waiting on Viola to cut him off. Are u taken? If I was I taken these fifteen minutes of conversation would have been cut into a two second convo. (giggling) I'm single, so of course you can call me. I can't forget to mention I have no kids, I'm free!

Well great miss Viola I'm here to change that. Your very beautiful and I love your sense of humor. I will most definitely be giving you a call. Viola smiled back, wav-ing goodbye as Trey stepped into his ride. Her eyes read Ching Ching, he pussy instantly soaked, and her smile was as bright as the sun. she felt like she had found love at first sight.

What's going on Viola you seem a bit happy. Don't I suppose to be happy or would you rather this beauty to look beasty all the time. NOW Miya was one of spring fields finest. Very smart, many qualities and credentials. She graduated from Spring-field's university with her bachelors in fashion merchandizing. You guessed it, she was a designer. And of course, my personal stylist. She styled a lot of celebrities that lived nearby and numerous of upcoming artist in different states. Miya, had it going on. She didn't too much want for anything, on the count of her parents was rich as shit. Her pops were one of the city top executives who made 6 figures each year. Her mom lucked up and got pregnant, where she had met her pops at a bar in new jersey and fucked him the first night. He had to take on a big responsibility of having a child, so he paid her way through nursing school. I guess you can call that luck. Miya was very sophisticated. She only dated dudes who drove luxury cars and wore suits. She said, "the man that stand beside me needs to compliment me." she's one of the reasons I decided to change the way I treated men. I loved her cockiness and arrogance. Her standards were so high her heels weren't anything less than a thousand dollars. She drove a champagne pink range, & lived in 3bedroom condominium on the outskirts of Springfield's. You would have thought she had a roommate or even kids. It was just her; I guess that's what they call better living. Chatting over the sushi bar the girls conversed for an hour or two, discussed upcoming events, talked about what's new, what's old and whose dating who and other secrets. They hardly ever have time to get together due to work and

Elizabeth having to stay home. She was a real Springfield's house wife. She was the only one out of the circle. The perfect wife! She cooked cleaned, shopped, & took care of the kids. We called her 'super mom'! Elizabeth dated rapper Harlem. Harlem was one of Springfield's big-gest rappers. His music had a big Impact on younger kids. Although Harlem never rapped about his actual real life. He became a big deal over the years. Elizabeth was seven years older than me. I met her at a bar one Saturday. I couldn't help but notice her long jet black hair, blue eyes, and pearly white teeth. Her body was amazing. Knowing now that she had birthed two beautiful girls at the same time, didn't see any stretch marks. I mean she was absolutely flawless. With her dating Harlem, she stayed laced with all the latest designer bags and pumps. Her diamond ring was nothing less than five hundred thousand. She was half perfect as well with kids and all. The bitch was the shit, and that's all it took for her to capture my attention. I only hung around the best, those of my caliber and Miya & Elizabeth had it going on.

The bill please! We've been here for too long and I had to get back to work. The bill said four hundred dollars. I got this one it's on me! You don't have to tell us twice!! the ladies grinned! smooches ladies, I'll send you both emails on our next outing. Love you, toddles!

2am in Springfield... abruptly awakened by numerous of missed phone calls and voicemails it was Simone. Viola Immediately felt her stomach drop assuming something was wrong. Simone usually turns her phone off after twelve, those are her layup hours she spends with her boyfriend. Knowing her, she would have more than enough men blowing her phone up, thinking they were the chosen one. Something had to be wrong. Calling her cellphone back repeatedly, still no answer. I hope everything's okay. Viola couldn't sleep, just the gut feeling she had she knew something wasn't right. Viola turned on the television, finally dozing back off.

She woke up to the sound of lawn mowers and sunlight. Viola hopped out the bed, peeked over her condo balcony, it was sunny day! Usually around this time she would be getting ready to do her morning run, but it was Saturday morning, she wanted to go shopping instead. Due to a stressful week all the men, bills, and head-aches she had gained trying to get her life in order she treated herself to a massage and a new studded Celine bag. It was very exclusive, meaning she was the only one with it. Viola knew she'll catch a lot of side eyeing once she hopped out of her Benz with that one. Elizabeth didn't even have that particular bag, on the count of she owns more bags than Mrs. Celine herself.

Arriving at salon Dior, it was about a twenty-minute wait on her massage so she sat in the waiting room and fangled her fingers. Two women walked in the salon which had caught Violas eyes Immediately. Seeing that one woman had on the exact bag she had just purchased just an hour ago. Violas eyes opened in disbelief. She couldn't believe her eyes; she was somewhat mortified. "talking to herself" my bag was twenty-six thousand, who could afford that!! I mean I know I'm not the richest but my purse was exclusive. Where did she get it, it must be fake! Twenty-one questions running through her head at once. On top of the Celine bag, she's drop dead gor-geous. Long hair, she had to be at least 5'8. her posture was incredible. I'm thinking Americas next top model but I didn't want to overdo it. Then to put the icing on the cake I couldn't help but to over hear their conversation in which she sounded ex-tremely intelligent, school teacher came across my mind. The two women sat across from Viola she played with her phone trying to disguise herself as if she didn't eye the two from the moment they walked in.

"Niko told me he had another surprise for me after I'm done being pampered, I won-der what it could be.

He might want to take you to Hawaii, your birthday is next week."

NIKO! Viola thought to herself. It's not too many Nikos in the world. Trying to figure out if that could be his wife. He told me she had cancer, I doubt that's her.

...after the massages was over Viola and the women ended up leaving at the same time. Getting into a light blue Bentley with tinted windows...

HOW IRONIC. it was Nikos wife!!! she doesn't look like she has cancer at all. Was he lying to me? But why would he lie, she's incredible! I wouldn't even cheat on her, I mean she's a stallion.

CHAPTER 3

Viola sat by her phone hesitating for about an hour after getting the courage to call Trey. She didn't want to seem like a jump off that was desperate to talk to a basket-ball player, on the count of she knew he had a lot of fans. Not really knowing any-thing about basketball, before their first date she wanted to Impress him. She sat and watched sports center until she had the basis down to a science. Hey, you've reached Trey furgerson, I'm sorry I couldn't.... click! Viola hung up before the machine beeped. I absolutely hate when people don't answer my calls, now it's really going to seem like I'm desperate. When he calls back I'm going to send him to voicemail, and give him a call back three hours later just to make it seem like I'm busy. Child-ish, right?

Viola heard thundering as she walked over to the window to shut it. This is going to be a long night. I'm in the house alone, no wine, my power keeps cutting on and off, and on top of that I can't get out to make any money. This rain shit is for the birds. Laying in her California king bed covered in her silk robe. Viola still felt sexy even though it was loud lightening in the air. She really didn't feel so alone, she had her special friend. She used him every time she felt it was a sex recession, and there was definitely a drought due to the bad weather. Viola played with her toy for hours, even though it wasn't the real thing, she made sure she climaxed at least six times before she fell asleep. The next morning Viola met up with Elizabeth to discuss a few things. Waiting on her to arrive at joe's diner. She decided to get in touch with Trey, knowing she didn't have anything planned for the rest of the day, she thought maybe she could visit him, catch up and get to know each other more. He answered, he was very excited to hear her voice. He thought maybe she wasn't interested, for the simple fact she forgot to return his call the other day. So it's a date, send me your address and I'll be there to get you around eight. "cool, see you at eight!" Elizabeth arrived just in time seeming so sad. What's wrong? Viola asked, Elizabeth sat down in disbelief. Its Harlem, I think he's having an affair. An affair, Viola looked shocked! Yes, an affair! I'm putting all my clues together, and everything's adding up. I mean I never been so sure. Throughout our whole marriage, Harlem never stepped out on me. I gave him everything he wanted in a woman. I had his children and been the most loyal, passive, faithful woman to him. I never did anything to question the love he has for me because I knew the way he loved me was real and genuine. But lately for some reason I get the urge to go snooping and I saw things I never knew of. Me and Harlem talks about everything, from his studio time, tours, concerts, meetings, I mean everything. I know when he's eating, sleeping, hell I even know when his head hurts. I'm just so devastated. I keep myself up, I care about my wellbeing, my clothes stay on point. Hair always laid, house always cleaned, food always ready when he gets home and my sex is amazing. I make sure he gets is at least three times before I gets mine.

Okay now wait Liz, maybe your over exaggerating. Your thinking a bit too much. He's probably not cheating on you. He's probably just busy with clients and work. Viola, I said I went snooping meaning I seen the shit with my own eyes. You can't give a married man the benefit of the doubt. Wrong is wrong. Text messages are unacceptable. Phone calls at an unreasonable time are unacceptable. I wish I could come up with a reason he would step out on me, but I just can't name one. I've asked him repeatedly do he want me to come on the road with him, does he needs comfort-ing after a concert, massages, sex, heart to heart conversations. I was even okay with letting the kids stay with my mom for months to make sure I supported him one hundred percent. All I ever wanted was to be the perfect mother and wife to him and my daughters. Tears started falling down Elizabeth's cheeks while she went on and on about Harlem. Whatever you need Liz I'm here. I'm not married so it's kind of hard to put myself in your shoes. I can only Imagine the pain your feeling, but all I want you to do is make sure everything is accurate. Don't jump into any more con-clusions until you have the full facts. If I could keep it real with my girl, I would tell you the lifestyle he's living comes with groupies, fans, and women that's going to be throwing themselves at him every day all day. You're his wife, your number one. If he's stepping out on you it's not on purpose, it's not because your job at home is terrible and he's just tired of it. You're a great wife and mother. Him cheating just comes with the territory and with his lifestyle.

I'm sure he will never put none of those heffas before you. He wants you at home taking care of his kids. That's your job. His job is to make sure his family is good. So maybe sometimes he might have sex with a groupie that jumps on the tour bus, but that's just that. It's really nothing more!! Harlem loves you, he worships the ground you walk on. You're is everything and he will never jeopardize that. I know because I've had several conversations with him about it. So don't sweat it girl, don't provoke unnecessary arguments. If what I'm saying doesn't deliver to you, still just chill out for a second. Check for a change within him. If in weeks he's acting standoffish or like he's not interested anymore or don't care to have sex or anything in that aspect, then acknowledge the situation. But if everything's normal, let it ride!!!

See Viola its better said than done, but thanks girl I'm going to take everything into consideration and most Importantly pray about it. Wiping the tears from Liz's face. "that's my girl" that's why I love you so much, you're so strong! I know it takes strength to overcome obstacles, especially the ones we deal with today. But come on girl enough of that crying, you are making me mess up my makeup.

…. The clock read 7:45pm. Viola knew Trey would be pulling up at any time. Trying to fit her petite shape into her new extra small Herver dress. Staring into her long-studded diamond mirror she had just got. I hope he like my outfit, taking a sip of her wine. She received a message, it was Trey. I'm outside, Viola slipped on her charlotte Olympia heels Miya had bought her for a just because gift, swallow the last bit of her wine and took the elevator down to the lobby.

Trey greeted Viola so politely standing there with a dozen white roses. Wow this is nice! And you look nice, Trey said! Viola grinned, looking so turned on. I'm happy I could be your date to-night. Trey grabbed Viola and escorted her into the car. Trey was such a well taught man. You could tell he was the only child and a mommy's boy growing up. Very sensitive when he touches, polite, intelligent, and educated. The way he articulated his words made me feel dumb. He was the kind of man a single woman dreamed of having after her baby's father left her raising three kids. He was that superman. A ken to Barbie, a jay to bee. He was everything, and to top off all that greatness he was an athlete. "am I a lucky girl" Viola sat and mesmerized.

Arriving at Hudson's steak house. Pulling into a private valet service where only Bentleys Porsches and Maybach parked. The valet greeted me so nice and welcom-ing. You could tell Trey was a regular, on the count of he just threw his keys to the valet guy and grabbed my arm. Had me guessing "I wonder does he bring all of his women here." The way I stood next to Trey, I complimented him well. Thinking about my home girl Miya she would've loved seeing me on the arm of a basketball player. I can hear her now, "you go girl!!!" giggling to myself.

Me and Trey sat at the table for hours laughing and telling stories about our child-hood, and other great things. We really kicked it off, I could see us going far in the near future. My only problem was I couldn't get to attached due to the fact I live one helluva lifestyle, losing Trey would be the dumbest thing ever. Knowing if he found out about how I was living, he'll probably never speak to me again.

CHAPTER 4

She's here!!!

The next morning all I could think about was Treys sexy lips. I thought about giving him a call, but didn't want to seem so thirsty. Even though we hit it off well, he told me never to hesitate on calling him. I'm kind of surprise, well happy yet surprised that I didn't give him the goodies on the first date. Knowing that he's used to women throwing pussy at him left and right. I know for sure next time it's going down. Giggling to myself. Taking a step onto the balcony it was a gloomy day. I was completely free the whole day. What shall I get into? Trey is probably at practice and the girls are usually busy around these hours. I could go shopping but I had just about every piece of clothing, bag, and shoe that came out this season. I could go catch up on some of the new shows or movies, I said as I fell back into the massage chair. But I would be a loner. Gabbling on and on for about an hour, still with no plans. Two hours passed. I had fell asleep in the mist of my thinking process, but awaken by the doorbell. As I opened the door I seen no one was there. I looked down and seen a huge box fully tapped that read fragile. As I grabbed the package I struggled it to the kitchen counter. "this box is far from fragile" talking out loud. Slowly cutting one side of the box open with a razor blade, the box soon opened. Stuffed cotton was all over whatever was at the bottom of the package. It was a huge picture frame turned backwards. I was somewhat confused to who would send me a package. The address read unknown with no name stating who. As I turned the picture around, I instantly lost my breath. First thought was to drop it, but still in shock at what I was seeing. It was a photo of me and Niko naked at the room, BUTT ASS NAKED! I stared at the picture for about thirty minutes before I even thought about reaching out to Niko. I mean, "am I being punked, is this a joke, is Niko crazy as hell, or is my eyes just playing tricks on me. I wanted to believe that my eyes were just playing with me, but that's an unrealistic thought. Soon I ran into the room to find my phone. Scrolling through my text messages unable to find Niko's phone number. I'm an idiot!!! I don't save numbers, usually I delete my messages and my call log. I had to figure out a way to get in touch with Niko. I don't know where he works, I don't know what he does for real. I wouldn't think to ask knowing I wouldn't care, I just want my money.

Dammit. What could be his reasons really? I mean he did pop up at my house unex-pected. But it was a good deed. Maybe the house keeper was spying on us. "I will go beat her ass" but then again how would she know my address. The only person that knows my address was Niko, thanks to my careless ass. I didn't have too much more time to think on the picture situation. I had forgot once again that I had to pick up Simone from the airport. Since I had missed my flight to her, she said she's com-ing to me. Reasons why I love my best friend, even though I paid for the flight she still came. Arriving to the airport it was going on eleven o'clock. Simone had a late flight. I told her to get on the latest one due to traffic here in Springfield's, it's hor-rible here around five six o'clock. I didn't want to be stuck in all of that for hours. I just don't have the patience. I greeted Simone as I seen her struggling out the termi-nal with five suitcases. You would have thought she was moving in. HEYYY BEST-FRIEND!!! I missed you, Simone dropped her luggage, ran, and jumped into Viola arms. She had been going through so much with the death of her father and her crazy relationship problems. I told her she can come to Springfield's with me to get away from all those traumatic and negative vibrations. After we let each other go, I helped her carry her bags to the car. Simone was so loud and careless at times, she slung her leather bags any type of way into my backseat scratching up my leather.

Aye girl, be careful with those bags. The maintenance on this car is expensive. OH, SHUT UP! Simone straight faced Viola, u can afford three more of these if you wanted to. Speaking of afford I need help paying off some of these bills I got back at home. Simone, I just sent you two thousand dollars for that last month. What do you be doing with your money. Simone dropped her head. Girl I had to bond Greg out of jail. His dumb ass got pulled over in my car and didn't have a license, got my car Impounded. So, I had to pay for that and that! Simone, I told you about that. You need to leave him alone. He's a bum. He lives off you. He has four kids, he lives with his mom, oh and did I mention he was a bum? Like come on, you're too cute and worth so much more than that. Well yes, that's why I'm here to get away from all of that. I'm going to pretend like I didn't hear you going hard on my man. It's just sometimes it's not about the money when you really love him. He treats me right, so that's all that matters. Right? Simone said in a devastated tone. HELL NO! That's not right at all and don't let a bum tell you any different.

Pulling back up to Viola's condominium, Simone was so amazed at how her crib looked. When they were in high school they only vision life so beautiful, Simone never really thought Viola will be living so abundantly and she was really doing the damn thing. Viola I'm so proud of you. You got everything we ever wanted, every-thing we ever fantasized about. All it takes is hard work and dedication. Sleepless nights, you must really sacrifice your pride and dignity! Why your dignity? Simone asked. Listen Viola, go to the kitchen and pour us a glass of wine. Get the expensive bottle, because once I tell you how I get it done. Your either gone love me more or kill me. Simone stared at Viola so curious to know what she was about to share with her. As she walked in the kitchen, she started to ask question after question. As they sat on the couch, Viola starred in her eyes, trying to grasp her full attention, loyalty, and commitment. If I share this information with you, as my best friend you promise me you won't tell a soul. I mean not your bum of a boyfriend when you guys feel like pillow talking. Not your city friends that gossip for a living. You know if they found out anything about me and how I got paid the anticipation to tell will be real. I promise Viola, you know you my girl I'm with you wrong or right. I got your back tighter than my bra strap! Pour it out!

Now I'm going to run down my whole set up, my caliber of people, how my standards are set up, and how much of a boss your friend really is. I volunteer at a community center full of girls that look up to me, they admire me they want to be just like me. How cute is that right? Would you ever believe me "VIOLA" the bully in high school, the fighter, the loud mouth ghetto girl will become some one's idol one day. Well yes, I've done a complete 360 in that area. Well listen, I'm more than any woman can Imagine. My dreams, goals and aspirations have changed throughout the years. My ways of thinking are more complex but precise. I like to get things done. I'm more of a HANDLE THAT SHIT type of lady. If I want something, I grab it! If I need something, I take it! To be a boss you must be dominant. No one can tell you how you suppose to run your operation. No one can have opinions. No one is even allowed to talk when I speak. You see how you're giving me your full attention and didn't even bulge to interrupt? That's how bosses operate. I stand up straight, look you dead into your eyes to let you know I mean business. & I'm serious about my shit! My shade could be so real if I told you about other women in this city, but then I wouldn't be minding my own business. The most Important rule in this game is minding your own business. Never worry about whose hot, who's not! Whose dating who, whose fucking who. Stay persistent to what you do, and you will win! I took a night out on the town to peep out the sceneries. I wanted to get a view of the city. You know, see who was popping, who does what, and who was really making moves. I scoped out the hottest strip clubs. The hottest dispensaries and went to all the concerts. I met a few guys along the way who had there shit together and on point. They gave me a few pointers on how to deal with country men, but I'm talking paid men. I see you staring at me with a mortified look. How dare you thoughtlessly insult my character as a woman? I'm no gold digger, if that's what you're thinking. I just see a way to come up in a big city full of entrepreneurs, doctors, athletes, and drug dealers. Hell, I can feel bad intentions when I'm conversing with a guy. So why wouldn't I take what I can get. Moving along with the story, my innocent ways soon turned into a huge operation. It was my business. I made thousands a night. I kept myself exclusive and it was my price or no price.

Viola, are you a trick? Now Simone, I wouldn't call it tricking because I really got it. I'm real charged up out here. Look around, I'm living better than ever. I take care of my family. I pay all their bills; they would never want or need for nothing ever again. Moral of this story is, are you down or what? Before I let you answer, do I have to remind you how much of a bum your boyfriend is. How late you are on your bills, and how every week you ask me to send you money. Now answer!! Viola starred at Simone so serious and competitively.

Simone took another sip of her wine; can I think on it? Or do my bossy best friend need her questions answered right after she ask them? Laughing to herself... but re-alizing Viola wasn't in a playing mood at this point. Okay whatever, I'm in! Raising her glass, indicating a toast.

Get dress! Tonight, I'm taking you to dinner. Well really, I'm taking you to a steak-house where all the men of status eat. But we are eating too. So, get sexy. You can wear a dress from out my closet. Put some makeup on and smell like jimmy Choo tonight. Viola was extremely serious when it came down to her business. She didn't play too much when it came to her money. Simone was in shock seeing her silly bestfriend so serious for a change. She didn't know if she should laugh or really take her serious...

Going on ten o'clock. The girls arrived at Boston's steakhouse. As you know Viola had to make a special entry, waving to all the employees. You could tell she was a regular. For all the wrong reasons, but even the chefs greeted her with smiles. As they sat down, Simone wasn't used to upscale restaurants. Not only didn't she know how to order but she didn't know the difference between the steak fork and the salad fork. Trying to be so unlike herself, she grabbed the napkin flopped it on her lap, pulled out her mirror to check her lip stick and took a sip of her wine. Gradually a guy greeted the two of them. Simone was so used to being around her boyfriend she didn't know how to approach a rich man. She was instantly intimidated. Looking at Viola she had the conversation down pack, they were talking as if they knew each other forever. Hey, this is my best friend Simone, she's from Ohio. She up here with me for a while. Hello Simone, staring directly at his pearly white teeth. She spoke back with a shy calm voice. I'm Robert but all my boys call me Rob you are very beautiful! "Taking a seat next to Simone as he complimented her over and over." Viola loved the instant connection, she blushed as if she knew Simone had her first customer. Even though she was a bit nervous, hell she's grown, she knows how to talk to a man. After dinner was over, Viola waved her ticket in the air so the valet man would bring her car around. Rob and Simone hit it off, exchanged numbers, and gave friendly hugs goodbye. Blushing hard as ever, Simone jumped into the car. The conversation was quite odd. Due to the fact, all Viola ever heard Simone talk about was her boyfriend. Since though all fascinated her she could speak about was him and his clean sharp suit. Wow Viola, I could really get used to this lifestyle. I told you girl, it's time we go up, and this not even the beginning.

Miya this is my best friend I was telling you about from back home, Simone. Simone spoked back but stared at how beautiful she was. How perfectly her jeans fitted, and how intelligent she spoke. Simone felt as if she didn't fit in. For the simple fact, these girls in Springfield's had it all figure it out. From top to bottom. They were about their money and knew how to get it. I had to jump on the train as soon as possible. As of today, my confidence will be on another level. I'm not even going back home no time soon. Simone mumbled to herself for a good three minutes while Miya and Viola talked about shit she knew nothing about. It's on! Even though Miya and Viola was the complete opposite, at the end of the day the outcome was always income and that was enough for me to be apart. Women of their caliber was always on top. Miya was cute and had her shit together and all but it was something about her that seem a little fishy. I couldn't quite peep it out right off back, I knew I had to be careful of the things I said around her. I didn't want to judge her so soon because I didn't want to seem like a hater so I decided to let things play out. I was going to make sure Viola was very discreet with the way she moved around her.

After lunch that day Viola had to get back to work. She promised her neighbors kids she'll take them all out for ice cream last week. They wouldn't let her forget what she had promised them. She gathered all the girls up and drove them to the nearest dairy cow. It was only two girls that wanted to go out of six children, so she was kind of excited. As the girls arrived at dairy cow, Viola phone rung, it was Trey. He wanted to meet up with her that afternoon to have lunch. Even though Viola just left from lunch with Miya and Simone, she couldn't resist a date with Trey. She pretended as if she was starving to him on the phone. Okay, "I'll see you around four. Viola dropped the girls back off, and jumped into her ride. She flew home since though it was already three o'clock, she had to freshen up quick, she had plans on kissing all over him and bringing him back to where she stayed.

Viola met Trey at the sushi bar they seen each other at when they first met. This time he was dress down Balenciaga's on his feet, Balmain's for his bottoms with a ysl shirt to match. She couldn't resist the smell of men's creed flowing across his chest. As she hugged him, she moaned and licked her lips. Viola couldn't wait to end lunch; all she could think about was sex. She looked around to find a bathroom trying to figure out if he was spontaneous enough to fuck her in the girl's bathroom stall. She didn't want to come off so ready, but hell that's all she knew. Trey stared her in her eyes and bit his bottom lip. You are so attractive to me. All the things I would do to you. Shaking his head,

Likewise! Viola responded. I was thinking we could skip lunch and head straight to desert and that's about a thirty-minute drive from here if your down. Trey flagged valet around to bring his car back. Lunch is skipped, I'll follow you. They both jumped into their car and sped off. Pulling up to Viola's crib. Trey was very intrigued. Her place was astonishing. Everything was neat and do-mestic. Trey laid back on the couch while Viola poured wine. At four thirty? Trey asked. It's quite early and I only drink cognac. Just taste it, while I taste you. I always wanted to see how a basketball player felt anyway. Let me take care of you. Trey sipped his wine while Viola slid her tongue up and down his navel. Unbuckling his pants, she caressed his penis with her right hand and licked the tip of it. His eyes rolled to the back of his head as he moaned her name. Viola wanted to please him in a way she knew no woman had ever. She grabbed his hand and led him to her bed-room. After a few minutes of kissing, they both was naked. Viola grabbed his penis and pushed it inside of her, slowly riding him. As he gripped her ass she rode quicker. Viola wait, I'm about to cum, slow down! Viola sped up. Caressing her tongue on his neck, he let off a big one. Loud moans came from the both, breathing hard as they climaxed at the same time.

Wow, I never came that fast before. You must know something I don't know. Trey said as he pulled his pants up. I just know how to please what I like. Viola grinned. Don't be giving my vagina away to nobody, u hear me? YOUR VAGINA, this our first time having sex and its already your vagina, even though she was so turned on by his cockiness, she stared at him with a suspicious look. Viola had to catch herself. Knowing how cut she was when she talked to her customers she knew she had to be a little sweeter to Trey. Trey wasn't a customer she had to remember that. This pussy belongs to you if your penis belongs to me, whispering in Treys ear. Trey bit the bottom of her lip, "I'm all yours!!"

It was almost that time for Treys basketball game to start. Viola wasn't into sports, but anything for him. As she sat in the stands with Simone, they cheered on Trey as he ran out and shook all his fans hands. My baby look so sexy with them shorts on, I can't wait until he starts playing hard. Yeah yeah, Simone interrupted. Forget all of that, just make sure you hook me up with his friend Darius after the game. I must get my Clio up. Even though he's so fine, I might consider taking him serious. Wait now, I can't hook you up with nobody he knows. If what I did got back to that man, he will never speak to me again. I'm not taking that chance. Viola what do you think I'm going to do. Tell on us, I'm in it too. If they know about you, they know about me. Simone with all due respect, nobody knows you here. You wouldn't matter. But my reputation would be ruined. Let's just say you talked to his teammate, anything could happen, he could go snooping, he could be a stalker, he or you could possibly fall in love. Who knows. I just want to keep everything professional when it comes to our business. My love life and business can never clash. Well Viola, best-friend to best-friend he's going to find out eventually. Either that or you have to quit all of this soon. The minute you guy's relationship goes to the next level. He's going to want you home all day, acting like a wife, having babies, cooking and cleaning. You're going to be just like your miserable friend Elizabeth. Chile please, I got this under control.

Hey Viola!!! They were interrupted in mid conversation. How are you, what are you guys doing here? Viola looked shocked, it was Miya, seeing her at a game that's unlike her to even come to something like this. What are you doing here? Viola asked.

I'm here to watch my boo friend play. And who might that be? Viola Grinned so eager to know. His name is Darius Crawford. He plays a starting position, and you know me!!! I like those kinds. Simone peeked at Miya as if she said something wrong. Wow, and when did you meet him? Not too long ago, at the Versace store. I needed some new shoes, ran into him he grabbed the purse and belt to match also. Invited me to his game. And now I'm here. What brings you two here? Well you remember the new guy I was telling you about. Well he plays for the same team, and it's quite ironic how him and Darius are close friends. Really!! Miya said. Yes really, Simone responded back with a serious look. Yes, that is very ironic. How long ago was this? I just seen u yesterday and you didn't tell me anything about meeting an-yone. Trey scored in the mist of them discussing the two, Jumping and screaming, spilling popcorn all over the stands. The ladies were excited the hawks won the game. Leaving out the game, Viola met Trey in the locker room, walking pass secu-rity, no I'm no jump off, this is my man. Your man? So, you are claiming me now, Trey laughed. Yes, I'm claiming you, just like you claimed this pussy was yours last night. Laughing back. The guys in the locker room was all buck eyed as they seen how beautiful Viola was. She stood like a stallion. Aye, aye, this all me! Yawl carry on now, grabbing Viola by the waist and kissing her, he repeated, yes this all me! As they walked off, Simone stood on the wall with a furious look. She was still upset at the fact Miya talked to Darius. Trying to figure out a way to get to him without the help of Viola or Trey. She wasn't going to let up. Hell, she's not my friend, and she seems sneaky anyway.

CHAPTER 5

Something seems fishy. I can't quite put my hands on it. But something isn't right with your friend. My friend who Viola asked. Miya, she seems like a snake. Simone don't over react I know how you get, Miya is a cool chick. She's very standoffish, but that's just her personality. You just have to get to know her a little more. Yeah, I'll get to know her all right. I'm going to make sure I keep a close eye on her. Yes, whatever girl are you coming to the convention with us later or are you going to chill today, maybe use this day to go peep out the scenery, get to know a couple of people. Don't be so shy and up tight. Treat yourself to a drink a spa a movie or something. Its time you start making ends meet. What if I told you I was leaving for a couple of weeks. I need you to pick up slack. We don't do shut off notices or late fees, our bills are paid on time. I might leave town so I'm leaving all that up to you. So, get on your shit. Simone sat there fumbling her fingers asking questions after questions. Viola interrupted, no pity, no excuses, get on your shit! Ill check on you later. I have to meet up with my realtor, I'm thinking about buying another condominium too many people starting to know where I lay my head at. I can't live uncomfortable like that, so again

I'll call you later. Storming out, Viola wave goodbye and slammed the door. You have a collect call from "Greg" oh wtf, I can't take this... ignoring the call, throwing it on the couch. Simone headed to the bathroom, slipped her clothes off and jumped into the shower.

After thirty minutes of showering, she called her a cab. Viola wanted to teach her how to get it on her own without the help of anybody. Simone had to find her way and come up on her own. She showed her the ropes and how to play everything else was up to her after that.

Walking into a bar full of drunk men reaching for her hands, and grabbing her ass. Simone wasn't used to that much attention. She had to remember her job and how to get what she needed. As she sat by the bar her phone rang, it was Robert. She smiled from ear to ear, answering with a huge blush so excited to talk to him. Where are you, meet me at the bar on fifth street. Getting straight to the point, say no more, I'll be there shortly. As Robert arrived, Simone stood to greet him. I'll have two patron margaritas on the rocks. Drink after drink, soon the two was pilt. What are you getting into after this. Robert asked. I didn't have anything planned. Viola was out for the night, so I'm kind of just seeing what spring fields is all about. Do you mind hanging with me tonight at my place? Simone remembered what Viola said. Knowing she didn't have it in her to leave with strangers, let alone end up at their home. She was down. She followed Robert to his car, hesitating to get in, come on ma, I don't bite I just want to show you a good time while your here. I promise not to disrespect nor do anything you're not comfortable with doing. Seeing how much of a gentleman he was, she closed the door and they drove off.

I'm not a hoe. Excuse me! Robert looked at Simone with an awkward facial expres-sion. So, confused to why she would yell a statement out like that. I never said you were a hoe. I don't look at you like a hoe, you're beautiful too me. I'm sorry a million things running through my mind at once. I didn't mean to say that. I think you're a nice person. I just don't know what I'm doing in the car with a stranger. I'm just going to cut straight to the chase, I need money, so when we get to your house how much are you willing to pay. Robert didn't know how to respond to that question, due to the fact his intentions wasn't sex at all. Honey I'm not trying to have sex with you. But I am Simone interrupted. I said I need money. Either money or drop me back off to the bar. Robert sped up to busts a U-turn. I'll be more than happy to drop you back off. The car ride was silent as they pulled back up to the bar. Jumping out the car, Robert threw five hundred dollars at Simone and sped off. Simone looked back picked the money off the ground and smiled. Wow, that was quick!

Elizabeth stayed at Viola house with her two daughters for the night. Her and Viola had walked in in the middle of the night. Liz was crying, the girls were sleep and Viola was rubbing her back. Every time I see this girl, she's sad. Simone whispered to her. Hey Simone, Liz and her kids will be staying the night with us. Can you show her the guest bedroom so they can lay down, it was three am. What's wrong? Is everything all right, yes! Her and Harlem just had an argument, typical husband and wife behavior.

She didn't want her daughters around that drama. Harlem came in late drunk with lip stick on his shirt. Liz already assumed he was cheating so that kind of put the icing on the cake. But let's talk about it later I don't think she's in the mood plus its late. I've had a long night. You want to talk about long nights we will talk about my night in the morning. Simone added. Goodnight!

Simone woke up to Liz sitting on the balcony, it was sunny but a bit nippy. She was always a morning person, looking at the clock it was only 9 am. She slipped on her robe, poured Liz a cup of coffee and accompanied her. Hey girl is everything all right. Liz stared at Simone with a fist full of tears, no, nothing is okay, handing her Harlem's phone. She snuck it when she packed the girls bags last night. Harlem was so drunk he didn't even notice. After saying fuck this and storming out, he left his phone on the bed. Reading the text messages Harlem wasn't faithful at all. Every single message was females throwing pussy at him left and right. Simone had a loss of words. She didn't know how to comfort her, so she rubbed her shoulder and cried along with her.

When Viola woke up, the first thing Liz could say was she needed her lawyer to set up her divorce. Liz was so heart broken and dismayed she was ready to set every-thing up as soon as possible. With no intentions on making things right or even con-sidering counseling. She felt betrayed and disrespected. She wanted to start the di-vorce right then. I don't want to talk about it to him or no one else. I just want my peace, my kids and everything he owe me. I want my life back, screaming to the top of her lungs waking up the girls. She broke down. Mommy!! The girls ran to her arms as she sat on the floor in a puddle of tears. I can't let my girls see me like this. I'm a mess! Liz grabbed the girls and hugged them tight. Mommy loves you!

beep beep!!!! a loud horn kept sounding, as the ladies looked over the balcony and seen an old-school cavalier, it was Niko. Viola hesitated, why is this man stalking me once again. but realizing she couldn't get to upset that he popped up knowing he had some explaining to do after getting that anonymous delivery the other day. She wanted to find the underlying cause of everything. So, she was kind of happy for some reason he showed up. Not caring if Trey would've been there what he would've said or about anybody else that was wondering who he was. I'll be right back, rush-ing out the house with nothing but pajamas on. Viola walked up to the car. I was trying to get in touch with you, why haven't you called me. I couldn't find your number for shit. Who knows about us? Did you have somebody spying on us on the low, was it that Asian house keeper? Wait, pause! Tell me what is going on, Niko Implied. I got a delivery. Usually when I get deliveries its flowers, shoes, or fruit baskets, this delivery wasn't special at all. So, what was it, why are you taking for-ever to get to the point. Niko starred at Viola calmly but very eager to know what she was about to tell him. I got pictures of us goddammit. Naked pictures of us at that. Who could have been watching us. I mean was they up under the bed. Peeking through the window. I need an explanation. Listen ma, I got too much going on in my life right now to try an jeopardize it all and to go out my way to do all of that, don't sound like me at all. I want to see the pictures for myself. I burned them!!! Viola shouted, you think I'm about to save some X-rated photos of me, as if I'm proud to be having sex with a nigga name Niko that drive a blue Bentley. That type of shit doesn't pump me up. I'm mortified, but I will get to the bottom of this. Grin-ning at Niko, stepping out the car...and why did you even show up here anyway. What do you want from me. Viola added on. I wanted to take you out for Breakfast. I lost your number so something told me to stop by, I didn't think you would mind. Knowing that I already knew where you lived. I doubtfully thought it would be a problem. What kind of girl do you take me as. What we did was business, after business theirs no ties. You can't do this anymore Niko. Go play around with your sick wife. Make her feel better about life. Don't you ever come back to my house again, okay? Indeed! Niko responded as he pulled off!

Who was that Viola? The girls asked in unison. Just my realtor, I don't need yall up in my business this early though. I told you guys I was moving, he came by at his earliest convenience. But I have to leave asap now, shaking her head. It was just so many different situations going on, Viola had to take in all at once. At this point I need some clarity. I need to get a way. Reaching for her phone to call Trey.

I need a Break Trey, come on let's get a way, just the two of us. Can you take a vacation day from work? Babe the season just started, we practice every day and night there's no way I can tell coach I'm taking a few days off I will be suspended or possibly kicked off the team for the season. I'm mvp they need me to take them to the championships.

There's no way. But don't panic how about you and your girls take the weekend off. Paid trip to Hawaii on me. Just chill and relax, get your mind off of work and whatever else your dealing with. I got your back! I will answer every time u call. I love you. Viola paused! Seeming so blissful that Trey used the L word. I'm going to give you a call back later. Go book your reservations. Love you too, thanks bay. Viola responded.

Every minute since her conversation with Trey had been cheerful, she was nice to everyone after that point. Calling all her girlfriends to tell them the excited news. Ladies cancel all your plans this weekend we're going to Hawaii.,

CHAPTER 6

The girls met at baggage claim to get their bags, so happy that they were on vacation. We really needed this 'Liz Implied. All the mess with Harlem these hoochies, and the girls I just needed a getaway. Well it isn't like we needed the sun desperately we're already in it twenty-four seven. I just needed a nice weekend with my ladies, drama and attitude free. I know that's right! Miya high fived Liz. As the girls walked toward the exit doors. Viola spotted a familiar face she couldn't quite put her hands on who she was right at once but she seen her walking towards her direction. As she got closer Viola started to realize more of who she was. Soon it clicked, it was Nikos wife. She starred at Viola with the most devilish look. If a frown could kill, let's just say Viola would've been dead. Why is this broad staring at you like that? Simone confronted Viola so loud and ready to fight. Listen you guys, Liz interrupted. we haven't been here for two minutes yet and you all are already on tip. But did you see how that lady grimed Viola, I'm no fool' those were hate stares. I know a furious stare when I see one. Look ladies I don't know what that was about and I don't care! maybe she just liked my bag, I mean let's face it I'm used to women being upset for no

45

reason. Viola shrugged her shoulders and walked away. As the girls followed Viola to the Hawaiian transportation station they were picked up in a stretch limo. The driver politely opened the door handing each of them a glass of champagne followed by a bowl of strawberries to put in it. Such a gentlemen Miya mentioned. As the girls arrived at their hotel, it was real dark in the room. Viola opened the fully plush curtains to get sunlight into the room. Straight to the beach we go ladies, pull-ing a one-piece swim suit out of her Chanel luggage. Viola was so ready to feel the ocean breeze hit her legs while she sipped on her patron margarita. As they walked the strip Simone peeked at Miya seeing that she was very upset about something. walking closer to her she wanted to see what was wrong. What's up Miya is every-thing okay? Simone asked, not genuinely caring just wanting to be nosey. Nothing, it's just work! my assistant didn't tell me I had a meeting with one of the top execu-tives of Springfield tomorrow. That was my biggest deal yet. That meeting with him would have took my business to the next level. I'm pissed because no flights are going back to Springfield tonight, I'm going to just take this as a lost and enjoy the rest of my vacation. The girls all rouse to toast to a blessed and prosperous year.

Walking to the concession stand that was place in the center of the resort, Liz went to get her another drink. This was her seventh drink. she tumbled across the beach chairs so clumsy and intoxicated. As Liz got near the bar she looked over and seen the same two women that stared Viola up and down at the airport. The women didn't recognize Liz was with Viola so she sat directly next to them. Budging in on their conversation but acting completely uninterested, Liz over heard the women venting about her husband Niko and how she thinks the girl she seen at the airport was the same girl on the photo some suspicious person sent to her house. Liz tried to despise herself pulling the drink menu closer to her face. "she couldn't possibly be talking about Viola" on the count of she knew Viola would never have sex with a married man and take pictures of them then purposely send them to his wife. She must have her confused with another person. Liz thought to herself as the bartender handed her her drink. Liz didn't want to mention anything to Viola until after the trip was over. She didn't

As the girls prepared themselves for dinner. Trey called. Hi baby, how is your trip so far? It's going well, I'm having the time of my life. I needed this, I owe you one A big long one if you know what I mean. Viola giggled. On a greater note, the girls are getting alone. We are about to head to dinner now. I'll send you a selfie soon. As Viola ended the call another call was waiting...It was Niko!

What part of leave me alone doesn't he understands. knowing his wife was at the same resort she was at, was probably the reason he was calling. Viola thought but still Ignoring the call again as he repeatedly called. I don't know what these two are up to but I won't any parts in it.

After dinner Miya and Liz raised their glass to thank Viola for the trip. They only had a day left to spend in Hawaii so they wanted to make the best of it. After a few more shots of vodka and laughs the girls exhaustedly headed back to their rooms. Go head, I'll catch up with you guys in a minute. Liz shouted out as she walked in the opposite direction. Dazing off into the ocean, the breeze and the waves sounded so peaceful. All Liz could think about was Harlem. As tears rolled down her cheek. she started reminiscing about the good times they shared.

In the mist of her day dream. Liz heard a phone ring, she walked toward the sound, she seen it was Viola's phone. She didn't want to answer although the person that was trying to get through never hung up. A text message popped up on the screen with an unknown number that said Please answer, its Niko!

I can't believe Viola would mess around with a married man after all the bullshit I'm going through with Harlem. Pacing back and forth beside the hotel door, before Liz walked in she had to manage her composure, she didn't want the girls asking her what was wrong, so pumped and agitated she knew she would've blurted Violas business out. I mean do I must question who she is as a woman now. Liz thought to herself, knowing Viola stood for woman power all over the world. I told her all my problems, she gave me the greatest advice, but wasn't living by what she preached. I was going to lose my husband and my friend.

The next morning the girls gathered for Breakfast, it was there last day in Hawaii. Did you guys see my phone? Viola showed up to Breakfast late looking for her cel-lular device all morning. Yeah girl I seen it on a beach table last night as I walked the strip. I was going to bring it to you but didn't want to wake you. Handing Viola her phone as she sat down she looked through her phone and seen several messages. Since though, one of her messages was opened and read. Taking a quick peek at Liz, she almost had a clue

Liz had went snooping through her phone. Viola didn't want to ask her. She didn't want to make It seem like it was a problem that her friend read her texts, so she let it ride! I'm so happy I have true friends. I don't have to question their loyalty or friends I don't have to think twice about. Raising her mimosa initi-ating a toast, Liz concluded thanks for being wonderful friends. Taking a sip of her drink, biting down on a blueberry waffle, Viola giggled, I wonder if she's being funny because I'm not for the funny insiders, if she wants to take it there, I'm hilar-ious. Expressing a fake grin as she peeked back at Liz.

Okay ladies let's wrap this brunch up, this is our last day let's get drunk as hell and forget about everything we were ever worried about. Simone said in a vibrant tone.

Hey girl what's up with you is everything okay, you seemed a little down last night. Viola asked Liz as they walked away from the table. Yes, I'm great, just wanted to clear my mind. Liz responded, "pulling away from Viola" oh okay well you know if theirs ever a problem you can talk to me. Viola said as she walked toward the beach.

The girls landed back in Springfield. It was an ugly day that evening. It seemed as if lightning hit the city, for some odd reason everything seemed so out of place. Viola took the elevator up to her floor, grabbing her luggage. In the mist of her struggle, her phone rang. Trying to multi-task, she felt so discombobulated. As she opened her door slowly, she dropped her phone and bags. Her mouth dropped to the floor, seeing her furniture ripped and cut up, glass broken, water over flowing over the counters and blood spots all over her bedroom floors. Viola didn't know if she wanted to call the police or drop dead. Her stuff had been ruined and she didn't have a clue to who it could've been. Opening her closet her clothes had been bleached, and all her jewelry was missing from out her jewelry box. Viola grabbed her safe key the moment she noticed fingers prints all around her safe. Fin-gers shaking as she nervously opened it. Her eyes widen happily seeing that all her money was still there. She fell to the floor in tears, as she dialed 911.

Police asked Viola question after question. Ma'am do you know who it could've been? When and what time this could've happened? Do you have surveillance cam-eras? Excuse me Sir, she interrupted, if I had a clue of that do you think I would have called you. I just got back in town. I don't know anything. Can you look for fingers prints or maybe go ask the information desk to see if they seen anybody looking suspicious walking out this weekend. I mean can you do your job? Viola said in a rude tone.

I'm sorry miss I know this is a difficult time to converse about something so tragic, but in order for us to do our job we need you to cooperate. Viola wasn't trying to hear it. She only called the police because she knew that was the right thing to do. She already knew they was going to give her the hardest time of her life. They couldn't do shit for her. Okay, I'm sorry I wasted your time but I'll handle it from here. Thanks! Rushing the officers out of the house and slamming the door insanely hard after them. Viola didn't know what to do, who to call or what to say at this point. All she could do is find somebody to come clean all this mess up before Simone showed up. Speaking her up, Simone walked in stepping all over broken glass and wet floors. What the hell happened here? Are you okay? Simone instantly thought Viola had lost her mind and decided to ruin her crib. Why is there blood all over the place? Simone asked nervously. Clearly, we had been robbed. They broke into my crib and destroyed everything. Please don't ask who because I honestly don't know. In mid conversation Viola spotted a mini note written on the wall next to the balcony. "THIS WHAT HAPPENS WHEN YOU SLEEP WITH MARRIED MEN"!

Simone eyes widen, well at least you know it was some jealous broken hearted bitch that don't know how to keep her man in the house. Viola tried to gather up her thoughts, they were all over the place. Who could have done this? As she burst out into tears, Married men!!! I only fucked one married man. And the wife was at the same resort as me. Wife! Simone repeated, yes wife. The lady that you were arguing with at the airport that stared me up and down was the wife of the guy I slept with. In which, I didn't have a clue he was married. But the minute I found out, I was so caught up in getting my money I didn't care after that. Now one thing I don't do is sleep with married men you know that Simone. But business was business and I told him to never call me again. I don't know why this situation is following me every-where I go. I can't catch a Break. I just don't understand how she could know where I live. I know Niko didn't tell her. Even though, he had popped up here on several occasions. Well there you have it. Simone interrupted, she must've followed him. If a wife senses her husband cheating don't you think she's going to go beyond to find out who what when where and fucking why?

Let's get this shit situated before it gets out of hand. Don't let this bullshit tamper with your business or with your man. Trey!!! Viola had forgotten she was supposed to meet up with him after she landed.

Picking up her phone, she had twelve missed calls, a few from him and an unknown number.

Trying to freshen up a little Viola slid on a sundress and some Chanel sandals, reached for her car keys and jetted out the front door.

Pulling up to Treys crib, he was standing on the lawn happy to see her. As she got out the car she ran to him and wrapped her arms around his neck to lean in for a kiss. What's up love! How was your trip? Did you enjoy yourself? And why you look so agitated. Viola didn't want to tell Trey about the Break in. She knew he would ask a million questions that she knew she couldn't answer honestly. So, she just pro-claimed on about the trip. I had a great time. I appreciate you so much you just don't understand. I want to do something special for you. WAIT! Trey cut Viola off. I got something for you. Another surprise Viola smiled from ear to ear. Trey you've done enough. No don't say that. Too much is never enough for a queen. You are so beau-tiful, smart, and strong from the moment I laid my eyes on you I knew I wanted you to be mine. Stuttering over his words Trey was extremely nervous, as he got down on one knee he pulled out a box. As he opened the box, Viola took a step back. Trey, I know you're not about to do what I think you're about to do? Eyes widen as tears started to flow. Would you marry me? Would you take this journey in life with me? Could I have you, to cherish you, to honor you, and to bring nothing but constant joy into your world? YES!!! Viola shouted out. The nosey elderly neighbors walked towards the sidewalk and applauded the new engaged couple as they hugged and kiss.

I'm engaged!!!!!! Screaming into the phone, Viola had reached out to Simone, Liz, Miya, and her mom. Engaged, Simone was in complete shock. Due to the fact, she just had the worst incident of her life. Thirty minutes later you're engaged. Yes, I know he just proposed. Simone sat on the phone quietly. How and why did you accept that proposal? You are already in enough bullshit. Your lifestyle isn't typical wife behavior. Yes, Simone I know what you're thinking, but trust me I got this under control. I'm going to get to the bottom of everything first thing in the a.m. Even if we had to go back to our savage days and put the hoe to rest, let me just enjoy this moment. I love him and he loves me. Can you just be happy for me, PLEASE!! Just this one time, Viola sobbed! What do you mean, this one time? I'm always happy for you I got your back tighter than your bra strap. I just want you to be careful, this isn't you! You are engaged to a basketball player this is a big fucking deal. Meaning you are going to be public with him. All on the blogs and media take-out, I don't think you have a clue to how major this is. Wait! Are you going to stop our business? Speaking of business, how you gone put me on this dope ass operation then bail out on me. I was just getting started, my clientele is already colossal and it's been what? One month! Simone ranted on and on. First off, pause bitch! This doesn't mean I'm going to stop getting money. Can't a man stop my money he's just adding to my account. If anything, he should love a woman with her own ends that can bring more than pussy to the table, plus I like him. He makes me happy you know I never had that before. I will tell you this this shit is between us so keep it confidential. Now that I'm engaged to Trey you're right the media will start follow-ing me everywhere I go. Make sure you are discreet with how you move. Seeing you with me, eventually they will start to follow you. We don't want that much attention on you. Until I figure out how I'm going to keep my pussy tight every night for my fiancé' while I fuck random niggas. I need you to move more carefully. Simone chimed in. Speaking of moving carefully, What's the plans for this Niko's wife chick? I can handle her if you want me too. I'll call my girl join up and we will get her for you. You don't need to handle anything right now Simone. We don't even know if that's her. We'll damn, how many more married men have you had sexual intercourse with? Viola laughed, BITCH! I hate you. None that I know of, they both laughed as Viola ended the call to call her mom back.

That girl is a hot ass mess. Viola giggled to herself walking back towards Trey. Her phone rang again. But the number showed up private she sent them to voicemail and grabbed her fiancés waist. Bay I love you so much! So, what now? Viola asked" well you know I have us something nice planned. Covering Viola's eyes with his hands don't open them until I tell you to. On the count of ten one two three they both began to count. When Viola opened her eyes, she saw a crystal blue range rover pull up with a white bow on top. Jumping up and down in excitement, Viola started to yell obnoxiously. Running towards her brand new 2017 range rover, she opened the door. Roof Roof' a Yorkshire terrier jumped into her arms with a gold name tag that read bella. My oh my Trey you are the absolute best this day couldn't get better. But it can and it will. Every day for the rest of your life, Trey smiled as he hugged his soon to be wife. Let's go get dress. Come on Bella. Grabbing her new puppy, she headed in the house. Dinner was nice. This entire day was perfect. I'm so flattered an at a loss of words, you've made this day so special I don't know what I can do to show you how grateful I am for you. Viola hush, you deserve it. Rubbing his fingers through her hair, Trey started to suck on her neck. Baby this feels so good, unzipping the middle of her dress falling backwards onto the California king bed into the five thousand count sheets. They were soon butt naked. Daddy let me take care of you turning Trey around, she went low towards his testicles. Licking and sucking one as she massaged the left ball with one hand. Spitting so much saliva on Treys penis, she started to suck the tip and penetrate his balls with both hands. Viola was a pro at what she did she studied pornos before she left to go trick off. She bit Trey stomach until she reached his neck. Lift up! She whispered in his ear, Viola had climaxed while she sucked Trey up. She squirted what she had left on the tip of Treys lip, then leaned downward to lick it off. Grinding her body on his she sat her vagina on the tip of his penis and rode him Kentucky derby. Loud moans from Trey as he screamed Violas name. Bae, you got it, you're going to make me cum. I love how you ride my dick, your what? Viola put her finger in his mouth. I love how you ride your dick, louder moans blurted out as he climaxed.

DROP TOP COUPE for a rich bitch. Simone blurted out! Rich bitch huh? Joi said yes rich bitch, I'm officially in and on my shit. I told you girl once you raise your standards it becomes levels with everything you do and touch. You'll be able to come to car lots and jump into whatever your heart desires. I still see commas in my bank account. I'm no longer living with Viola, I elevated. I put twenty thousand dollars down on a crib in belle land county, top security. I'm a big mama now! Speaking of big mama, I know your ass is tired of living with your grandmother. Wait! Was that shade? Joi checked Simone. No, no shade at all I'm just saying. I need you not to just say shit to me. I need you to know the only reason I'm with my grandma is to take care of her. Joi had to defend her situation. Simone had gotten big headed, just before her eyes she was acting just like Viola and her friends. Stuck up ass suburban bitches, Joi rolled her eyes. Dang girl I said no shade, you don't have to get mad at me. All I'm saying is you should jump on the bandwagon. Get you some of this El-Ludo. Giggling to herself, she had no remorse on how she just tried to play her friend. Simone was so caught up in herself she didn't even apolo-gize. She remembered her mom use to call it that every time she made her walk to the corner store for a pack of cigarettes. She used to say, "make sure you bring back all my el-Ludo" that was her change in her language. Knowing her daughter, she knew Simone would had tried to keep what was left from her ten-dollar food stamp. It's so much money in this game girl. I had to learn now it's your turn. I watched Viola pull up in all kinds of cars. I watched her shop until she dropped. I'm not going to lie the lifestyle is fulfilling and intriguing to me. The only thing is this must be between me and you. If Viola knew I told anyone about it she would kill me. Come on Simone even if I didn't consider I would never discuss this to anyone. You my girl!

Simone and Joi was on a mission to see who broke into Viola's condo. Simone couldn't and wouldn't let that shit slide. She was so determined to whoop her ass or at least threaten the chick. Hell, if she had the balls to call someone to do something so tragic, she can take an ass whooping. I know these Hollywood bitches never seen a belt growing up a day in their life. As they both ranted on and on, pulling up to a convenience store Joi grabbed a buggy. She tossed duct tape, a mask, rope and lawn scissors in the buggy and proceeded to checkout. Hoping back into the car, the girls pulled off.

I can't believe I'm getting married!! Viola pasted back and forth, trying to figure out how she was going to quit her night job. Knowing her and how hard she worked, she knew she had enough savings to last a couple of years. I mean if she invested it correctly. In which that didn't matter being Mrs. Ferguson she didn't quite worry about anything. Just the thought of waiting and depending on a man was too much to bare. I mean being a housewife couldn't be that bad, I can cook, maybe straighten up a little. Viola talked to herself as she continued to paste. I know he doesn't want my fine ass to do a full spring clean. Lord knows I barely does my own laundry. I got to give it more thought. Wait! More thought? Realizing she had already accepted the proposal. This is reality, my reality. I want kids, but I don't want them now neither do I want stretch marks. I most definitely don't want to wipe no shit. Hell, I barely like wiping my own ass. Let me just find Niko and get the air clear with his psycho of a wife. I sure do hope it was her that broke into my crib, deep sighs came from Viola as she dialed Nikos number. Hey, you've reached Niko, Viola thought to leave a message but hung up before the machine beeped. Viola got in the car, sat in the driveway for forty minutes until she got the strength to walk inside. In the mist of her gathering her things up, she had a call waiting from Simone. Bitch are you ready? "Ready for what?" Viola said. Ready to go lay this bitch down. I got joi with me we're ready. We already got the supplies we need and now we're headed in your direction. Viola thought to herself, why not I got to handle it someway, now, or never. besides Niko didn't answer anyway. I'll be ready in five minutes give me a second to change my clothes. Jumping into Simones new ride. who car? Viola looked shocked but pleased. It's mine, I just got it, you like? Do I like it I love it, this is dope. This shit here has a statement written all over it. Fuck this fancy talk. I'm ready to get this over with, what's her address. About that I don't have her ad-dress. Viola fangled with her fingers. I told you to give me a minute to figure things out. You so eager for action, you didn't let me get a chance to get the address. I know her sister works at fantasy stay, but I'm clueless to how she looks. Well what good is that going to do us blondie Joi smartly responded. Niko dialed in as the girls plot-ted. NIKO!!! hey Viola what brings you to my number. The last time I talked to you, you told me not to call you anymore. Yeah yeah small talk. This is big talk. Your wife destroyed my home then wrote a message saying " I shouldn't fuck women husbands" I thought this shit was over. Look, I'm so tired of you and your bullshit concerns you don't have to worry about her I got her. She's clueless, she knows nothing about you. Whoever else dick your sucking wife destroyed your home, not my wife. Since when do you care about your wife, sounds to me like your taking up for your Sick Wife. In which she doesn't look sick too me.

You have serious issues Viola. Your problems are going to hunt you sooner than you think. You fuck men for a living when things like this happens to you, its karma. Rather it was my wife or the next man's wife, its karma. Just be careful. Why do I have to be careful, are you threatening me. Threat!! I know that sick bitch not threat-ening you. Simone shouted out in the background. You want to speak about karma just be prepared for yours when it comes, you not a saint yourself Mr. married man. Niko hung up as Viola went off. GREAT! We wont find out where she lives now. Viola think about it. That's his wife, he wasn't going to tell you anyway. like DUH bitch that's where he lives. The next time he calls just be nice to him, fuck him again, apologize for going off on him. I mean I know you got a cold mouth piece you can talk his draws off in minutes. Then that's when we follow him home we can post up outside the crib until she pulls out or up and tag her ass. Cancer and all, I don't give a shit. She deserves to get the cancer beat up out of her we can do her a favor. The girls laughed at how serious Simone was. You are insane girl there's like no mercy with you. I'm just trying to get to the end of all of this so you're able to enjoy your engagement in peace. If all that got back to Trey he would kill you. Let's kill her and everybody else that has a problem and continue to get this money. Viola felt like she needed another vacation right after she had just got back from Hawaii. This is just too much, remembering she still had to meet with another customer tonight.

Trey and Viola debated about jointed accounts for about an hour. Viola thought he was rushing it a bit too much. We aren't officially married yet you sure you want to do that. Knowing Trey, you couldn't have told him that he was all in. He loved everything about Viola. He knew had plans on being with her forever, so why wait he thought. There aren't any secrets I need to know of is there? No babe, I just think we have forever to worry about all of that. Let's do things the right way. I don't want to mess this up. I love you. Viola knew she had to say something clever and worth listening to get him to understand. He's very hardheaded and smart. He can smell a lie and bullshit from a mile away. Babe, there are no worries, no secrets, it's just us. Let's grow and fall deeper in love day by day. Trey grabbed Violas face, it's too late I'm already there. You got me. I want kids I want a fairytale life with you. Let's take it there. I made a big step, I seen something unique and special about you the minute I laid my eyes on you. It wasn't that big ass booty or that amazing smile it was your intellect. I love and admire you baby just promise me you will never hurt or leave me. We can work out anything just be honest to me always. Now Viola was used to guys crying and sobbing all over her pussy, but Trey seemed as if he was fatal over her. She never knew a guy of Treys status would be so damn sensitive. Kind of annoying! Viola loved for her men to be all over her but Trey was the epitome of clingy. That only gives me a reason to dog him. Pay me no attention, ignore me, tell me to shut up Viola talked to herself, but Trey was the complete opposite. He paid me all the attention. Even while he played ball, he blew me kisses and wave every five seconds. He listens to everything I got to say even when I discussed the dingiest most irrelevant things. He was so into my thoughts, feelings, and emotions I didn't know if I liked it or not. Now I'm questioning my engagement thinking to damn much, was Simone right? Am I rushing things, will he find out, will this lavish life-style of mine be ruined and my business will be broadcasted? Increasingly questions cluttered Viola mind as she continued to overthink. It's up to me to keep shit in order, I'm the head bitch in charge. I run shit. The hell am I worrying about?

Trey had three more games left in his season and Simone still haven't bumped heads with Darius. She was determined to backdoor Miya because she hated her that much. Besides she was stable and had it going on now so it wouldn't be so hard to grasp his attention. Without Viola cock blocking she had to find ways to go around her. After another win, they all celebrated at Squids Crab House. Simone plays as if her phone was dead to use Treys phone. Trey was so intoxicated that he didn't realize his phone was laying on the edge of the table. Simone grabbed the phone scrolled through the contacts to get Darius number then quickly set the phone down before he turned back around. She sent a text "look to your left" Darius read the message with instinct reaction, turned to his left. Simone waved with a flirtatious grin on her face.

CHAPTER 7

Treys season was almost over and I still haven't had time to figure anything out. I felt as if my life had been falling apart but elevating right before my eyes. Trey will be on Break for a while, meaning he's going to want to spend overtime being up under me. Why didn't they make it to the play offs? Why do he have to be up my ass all day. Viola was good at overthinking a situation, the reason her stress levels was so high. She had amply amount of time to get her life in order, well at least that's what she thought. She also knew she was that bitch. Being that bitch consisted of never getting caught, never falling in love, and never getting played. We don't fall off, we don't settle!! In my case I wasn't settling I was winning but my lifestyle didn't match or balance my soon to be reality. Finally realizing I didn't mean to say yes and if I told Trey that he'll kill me. Miya had planned an evening for us both to meet and talk about the wedding. Ever since I told her about my proposal she's been my best friend. I don't know if she cares about the wedding or if she's doing it just to stay close to Darius. People have hidden agendas so you will never know. She had plans to reap the benefits of whatever Darius had to offer I'm sure. Knowing her, she must think I'm a little slow due to the fact Miya was always busy and stand-offish. She only came around when she could make time. Bougie bitch! She never had time to hang out or even meet on an everyday basis. Especially to talk about a wedding, I'm thinking she'll say send her an email on what's coming up but to make time yeah something had to be up. She had to think I was dumb. The bitch just wanted to get close with Trey to stay connected and on good terms with Darius. They weren't just teammates they were like brothers. In the back of my mind I'm thinking like bitch don't try to befriend my man to keep an eye on yours. The things women go through to get and keep a man me on the other hand really didn't give a shit.

I wonder what's been going on with Liz I haven't talked to her since the trip I didn't get a chance to share the good news with her. Which is so unlike her to not call me, I'm sure Miya told her anyways but still. Liz called me every day all day on and off the hour. I'm sure her and Harlem patched things up. Knowing him he probably bought her the latest whip begging her for forgiveness. I need to reach out to her. I felt that she had something against me. The tension in the room at Breakfast that morning was too uncomfortable. I don't know if that's still her problem but I 'll call and see. Hey Liz, its Viola. What's up chick! Liz spoke …Chick? Viola laughed. Liz never talked like that a day in her life. Something had to be on her mental. I was just calling to check up on you, I haven't heard from you since Hawaii. Is everything okay? Do you need anything? How's the kids and Harlem?

The kids are fine Harlem is Harlem and I'm great. Liz was so quick and dry rushing to get off the phone. Well I was calling to share some great news with you. Your friend is getting married. Yes, I heard, congrats to you and him. Liz softly responded. Viola stared at the phone feeling the vibe wasn't there. Liz didn't seem quite excited. Rushing Viola off the phone I got to go I'll talk to you later. Click, Liz hung up in her face. Viola was somewhat curious to why she started acting like that suddenly. Liz was like my sister. She had to go snooping in my phone, but even if that was the case I don't see a reason for her being mad. Rolling her eyes, everything will come to light soon.

After a quick nap, Viola woke up to the news, grabbing the remote turning the volume up. Rapper Harlem had been shot six times on Springfield's north side. Viola eyes widen as she fumbled with her phone. Trying to reach back out to Liz there was no answer. I have to make sure he's okay. I know Liz is sick. Simone dialed in as Viola slipped a Victoria secret jogging suit on. Hello Simone, Simone can you hear me. Yes, girl, did you hear about what happen with Harlem? Yes, I just watched the news what's going on. Liz shot him six times in the chest they don't know if he's going to make it. Viola heart felt like it had been rolled over by a semi-truck. He's at the medical center near midtown. The police are surrounding their home looking for Liz but she isn't there. OMG I just talked to her earlier she didn't sound like she wanted to be bothered I tried to talk to her and she hung up on me. I'm about to give her another call. In the meantime, meet me at the medical center in twenty minutes.

Simone and Viola arrived at the hospital at the same time, a city full of fans were surrounding the doors crying screaming and going crazy. Of course, I knew if Liz was the one behind the shooting she wouldn't have been there, looking to my left seeing Harlem's mom grieving in complete disbelief with the news of her son, hold-ing Elizabeth kids. I couldn't too much watch the poor lady break down like that. I didn't want to console her due to the fact I'm Liz's friend. There was no telling how she was feeling about her in that moment. A couple of hours went by and still no answer from Liz. In the back of my mind I thought Liz had skipped town, I mean if I would have shot my husband six times why would I stick around to clean up the blood. I'm out this bitch too. In the mist of my wicked thoughts it was going on two a.m. and rapper Harlem was pronounced dead. A soft-spoken woman walked on the side of me as I grabbed my things to go. I couldn't too much stomach sitting in the hospital no longer, I mean I knew Liz wasn't coming and Simone was laid across the chairs sound asleep. As I turned around the lady politely introduced herself. She sounded like an angel from heaven so sweet and innocent looking. Now I'm won-dering why in the hell was she trying to talk at a time like this then I thought maybe she was one of his family members showing her condolences. Hello I'm Viola. I know who you are, you are friends with Harlem's wife Liz. I stopped to look around making sure no one heard I was Liz's friend. No fake shit I just didn't want to fuel the fire that was already exploded in the waiting room.

My name is Kelly, I'm Harlem's baby mother. Our baby is a month old now. Viola eyes widen in shock. A month old, Harlem really was cheating. I thought maybe Liz was overreacting she didn't mention another baby to me, I mean who would that's quite embarrassing. But still I thought maybe he dibbed and dabbed in a few women but to have a fresh baby, Lord I'm surprised. I told Harlem he was the father a couple of weeks ago. It's my fault for breaking the news to him like that after the baby was born. But I honestly thought it was another dudes baby. Seeing that my baby looked everything like Harlem, every feature I started to question who his father really was. Even his supposed to be father wanted a blood test. Finding out the baby wasn't his I then knew who the father was. I reached out to him he kept hanging up on me, he wasn't believing me, He just kept saying him and his wife marriage was already on the rocks and how she wasn't going to deal with no more of his bullshit. At that point, I couldn't be selfish but I couldn't just walk away or even put my child in a fatherless situation either. We both agreed to keep it a secret after the second blood test. He was going to give me five thousand a month and was going to come see him every chance he got. I agreed to the plan, However, it was selfish of him. I took some time to think about it and realized my son needed his father. Even if we would've played it like that eventually the secret would get out. You can't hide having a child forever, it was just dumb and it showed me his lack of responsibility as a man. He had to man up and take on his father duties. I'm wrong for being so careless with my body but I owned up to it now. It took so much out of me to have to tell that man he wasn't the father. He could've killed me.

Well look at what happened to Harlem! Viola blurted out, nobody has a father, a mistress, or a husband. Wait!

He had already said they were two seconds away from a divorce, in fact I had no clue he was married when I sexed him. He pursued me. It's not all my fault. The only blame I'm taking is the news I hit him with unexpect-edly. I'm not the reason behind his murder, I'm sure she found out way more before and after me.

I'm not blaming you, but may I ask why are you here I'm sure if you and the baby was a secret I strongly feel that your presence wouldn't be required neither would your absence be missed. With all due respect you're not Important, as a matter of that fact you're like a fan in every one's eyes.

I know you are angry and I know Liz is your friend so you can clearly say the things she would say for her. I just thought she would be here. I wanted to comfort her myself woman to woman. But you're right my presence isn't required. Harlem isn't here anymore so I will be gone now. Viola waved her hand bye as a tear fell from her cheek. Realizing the situation, she was already in herself. I could be the reason behind a man's death, I'm just like her. In fact, I might be worst and what's even sadder is that I still didn't give a shit. Right then and there Viola knew she was cut from a different cloth, a true savage with no feelings getting ready to marry a man with the lifestyle of a trick.

After Harlem's funeral, no one heard or seen Liz. Harlem mom was stuck with the kids. I stopped by to send my condolences, flowers, and made sure the girls didn't need anything. I mean Liz was still my friend which was so unlike her to just leave her children. She loved those girls wholeheartedly and even though we weren't on good terms I still hope she was all right. The things a man can make a woman do. Which is sad because we are the ones with the power, we got the pussy! Viola said to herself as she got back into her car.

I have to meet up with my fiancé in another hour to discuss the wedding I'll call you as soon as I'm done. Viola said to Simone as she hung up and threw her phone on the passenger seat.

(Meeting with Trey)

I still can't believe we are getting married. Trey kissed Viola on the forehead as they sat and sampled cakes. Whatever you want for your big day is fine with me, we don't have a budget for anything. Just swipe my card and it's paid for. Viola wasn't turned on by Trey's money anymore it was his charm and cocky confidence that she loved the most. Everything about him was amazing. She thought how stupid she'll be to give that up over a sleazy couple of dollars. So torn between being dependent and independent Viola brain was a complete wreck. As another cake sample was placed on the table Trey took his finger dipped it in the chocolate covered frosting and put it in Viola's mouth. Baby I can get used to being with you every day all day. You make me so happy, I feel so complete. Trey expressed his feelings, dipping his finger for another sample of cake.

I love everything about this man. He's just too damn soft. Every chance he gets he's telling me some love story. Meanwhile I'm trying to figure out if I'm going to meet Simone for this double date we have later tonight. I have no clue how I'm going to ditch him. I think it may just be a wrap and Simone was gone have to hold it down on her own, which was good due to the fact the men we were

Sabotage

meeting just signed a million-dollar contract with NIKE. We both can't pass up that lotto ticket. If Simone played her cards right we could really start our own operation, have women working for us. We would be like their madams. This business is easy if you have the right mouth piece. I mean even if you don't I can teach you. That's what I'm here for to teach and inspire but only the boss bitches. I can't get too jiggy with weak bitches it's just something about them that makes my stomach turn.

Trey phone rang in the mist of Violas daydream, bringing her back to earth. It was Darius cancelling their suit fitting appointment. He said he had something very Important he had to take care of so they had to reschedule until further notice. As Trey talked to him Simone dialed Viola in to tell her the exact same thing. In Simone case, she told Viola exactly what was going on. She was meeting with Darius later for dinner and cancelled their plans tonight. Viola was kind of satisfied that Simone broke the news off to her before she did. Laughing at the fact Darius just told one bold face lie to ditch Trey. Okay girl, I'll talk to you later.

Simone and Darius met at bishop park around 9pm that night just before the sun went down. He was so eager to know why Simone was pursuing him the way she was. She went out her way to get his number when she's most definitely aware of Miya and him.

Hey, how are you? Darius greeted her with a clean white smile. I'm fine, I thought you weren't going to text me back Simone responded.

I'm a man, it all seems like a set up if you ask me. I know you are cool with Miya and even though I'm dating her I still wanted to know what was up. Nothing was up Simone said. I just find you very much attractive, I like your style, I like how you play, and plus you turn me on. I can careless about Miya we aren't friends. I want you, I want you in ways no other woman wants you. Look how I broke my neck to get your attention. You are a remarkable guy and I feel like I can please every fantasy. It tripped me out because the minute I told Viola I wanted you. Miya comes along and tells us she's dating you. I could've got upset, but I thought Hell she isn't my home girl I owe here no loyalty what's so ever. So here I am taking what originally belongs to me. Simone played with his ego for a minute as she rubbed her body up against his. I got us a room a regency tonight, would you accompany me. Accompany you? Darius repeated, yes, I will!

I would love that right after dinner, or we can just skip dinner and get right to desert. Let's make this one night you will never forget. We don't even have to talk any more after this. I just want you so bad. How I know this isn't a setup, Darius stuttered. Because I don't have time to set up anybody, I don't play with things I want. Plus, I don't like Miya like that so I can give two fucks if her man is cheating or not. Are you coming or not? Simone got aggressive. In which turned Darius on.

I'll be there just send me the room number and after you have your dinner I'll be on my way. Sounds like a plan. Simone didn't care about him ditching dinner she wanted to freshen up and go have her a couple of drinks anyway before she puts it down on him.

Later that night Simone waited in the room wearing a pearly silk robe, with LA 'Perla lingerie underneath. Her hair was pinned up in a messy white girl bun with red lips and silver pumps. Darius knocked on the door. Simone wanted to please him in a way no woman has ever so she slid the key up under the door, rushed to the window and propped her leg up on the edge of the window seal. She felt so sexy and was in the right mood to fuck the shit out of Darius. Darius eyes was filled with hearts the moment he seen Simone. He was turned on by her sex appeal. Wow, is this what I've been missing out on? Darius asked, I told you I can dress it up and make it real for you. I can be whatever you need me to be. If you just let me. As Simone poured herself a glass of red wine. Would you like any she asked in a sexy monotone voice? Darius pulled a pint of Hennessey out of his man bag; I like brown hard liquor but thanks anyway. Simone pushed Darius chest making him lean back towards the bed as she sat across his stomach she started to grind on him. All the things I would do to you. I know how to make you feel good. I'm talking really good, as she kissed his right cheek and bit down on it, Baby have you ever stuck your penis in a fat wet pussy before? Have you ever made it squirt by just talking? Have you ever made a woman so ready to fuck you that she screamed your name and called you daddy? Sliding his pants off his dick was as hard as a rock. Simone scooted down to grab his penis she caressed the tip of it with her lips and massaged his balls with her left hand. Darius moaned uncontrollable, not able to stop it. He gripped Simone ponytail, Baby don't stop, he's about to cum. Simone sucked slower and deeper the minute Darius climaxed. Climbing on top of his dick he was still aroused. Simone knew she had to ride it obnoxiously seeing that he stayed on hard after he let off a big one. She reversed cow girl him followed by a sixty-nine and doggy styled position for a couple more hours. They both laid back on the bed breathing hard as ever. I told you, you were missing out on something you have never had before. Grabbing her towel heading to the bathroom to shower, Darius smacked her ass and followed her.

party time....

I don't know about you guys but I'm ready to get this bachelorette party started. The girls discussed a few things as they sat around the dinner table. Looking sad, Viola wasn't too intrigued with the plans they had made for her. What's wrong Viola? Miya asked, Repeated by Simone, yeah what's wrong? I'll be okay, I just miss Liz. Did anyone talk to her? she supposed to be right here with us. No, I haven't heard from her, I've been watching the news every morning before work but all they talk about is Harlem. I reached out to her a few times yesterday but no answer. I'm sure she is fine. Miya said as she took a bite into her well-done filet mignon. Yes, I'm sure she is fine as well Simone concluded.

As Viola sensed the tension in the air she couldn't help but laugh and finish her wine. Only she knew the reason behinds Simones pettiness.

Simone grinned the whole time the girls had dinner.

What are you smiling about! Miya asked Simone

You talking too me? Simone giggled. I'm just excited about the plans we are making. My bff is getting married, I'm her maid of honor and this is just a happy moment. I have a million reasons to be smiling, and besides life is just awesome.

As Simone went on and on. Miya's phone had rung. it was Darius, dismissing herself from the table. Hold on you guys I have to take this, it's my boo, grinning as she walked away. Whispering into Viola's ear that bet not be who I think it is.

And if it is him, that is her man why would you be upset? Viola smartly said

Because I had sex with him the other night. Viola spit up her wine as she blurted out. You did what? Be quiet, you are too loud. Yes, I had sex with him and I'll admit it was awesome. He played with my vagina all night. I mean he stimulated my body in all the right places. I told him "I bet you will love to have me in your bed every night, and guess what? he agreed. Simone bragged as if she wasn't foul. I mean she sounded so sleazy. Viola knew she couldn't judge her though, not only for her slutty ways but because she was her best friend. I just wish you would have kept that secret to yourself. I feel kind of shady knowing my bff is fucking my home girls man. Ugh let's just pretend as if you never told me. That's fine too, Simone said.

As the girls wrapped up dinner and headed to valet, Viola spotted a note attached to her car.

"don't think it's over" sincerely karma! What in the fuck? is this girl delusional, she's following me everywhere. turning around checking her surroundings. I mean if the hoe want war it aint shit to get it cracking!!! I'm getting real sick of this shit. Handing Simone the note. SAY NO MORE VIOLA! I'm about sick of this bitch too. If only I can get in touch with this chick.

What do she plan to do? sending me these threats, I don't take threats lightly. Baby girl that's an ass whopping. She's clearly trying to ruin me. Because she thinks I'm ruining her relationship. Once again, I'm not the reason behind his actions. He's a grown ass man. She's a lunatic if you ask me. These notes don't scare anybody. She's only making it harder on herself and her life. His dick wasn't even that good. Why this hoe tripping mone. Viola laughed as her and Simone pulled out of valet.

Later that night Viola had to get back to the money.

Meet me at loves gas station around 9 o'clock. I'll be in the red 18-wheeler parked on the side of the break station.

…We must make this quick, I must go. Honey you must go? why so in a rush? sliding his fingers up and down Violas arms. There's things I must get done. Let's not get too much in my business, looking around the truck Viola was so disgusted. Do you clean up in here? I can't conduct business in here I'm sorry. Viola smartly said.

Where else can we go in the middle of nowhere? Let's just get it over with, I have a bed in the back. I brought condoms so you don't have to worry about being unpro-tected. look in the glove compartment for lotion, I got everything we need. Plus, it's only going to take me 3 minutes to cum anyway. When I tell you I'm horny I've been driving this truck for hours. back and in forth from the west coast too east. I need you to take care of me before I go crazy. You don't want daddy going crazy now do you, kissing Violas shoulder. Viola took a glance at him so turned off as sweat rolled down his face. Gold teeth was shining in his mouth; his draws were turned inside out. Just pure country bullshit. I can't believe I'm doing this, this is a real settlement, meaning too silent that outburst but mistakenly saying it to him.

What do you mean? Isn't this what hoes do? excuse me, throwing the lotion against his chest looking for the door handle to leave. I mean you are fucking for money. that's what hoes and tricks do. You can't complain about a dirty truck when you yourself have a dirty pussy. zipping his pants back up. Viola pulled out her 4.5 aimed it at his head, I'm no hoe or trick I'm a robber today. Pleading for his life, no I'm sorry I didn't mean... Viola cut him off as she leaned the gun toward his head. He continued to plead for his life, Viola snatched the two thousand dollars he had on the bed and jumped out the truck. Running back to her car in full speed she rambled with her keys jumped in the car and drove off. I'm no hoe I'm a business woman talking to herself while she cleaned her finger prints off her gun and slid it up under the passenger's seat. After that moment, Viola felt herself pumped and ready for action.

Calling Simone, meet me at fantasy stay I think I'm ready to pay little miss angry bird sister a visit. Walking towards the front desk, Hi I would like to get a room for the night. just one night the lady nicely asked. yes, just for one night, Viola re-sponded. You look so familiar; I think I've seen you somewhere. (getting straight to the point) Viola talked to the two ladies not knowing which one could be her sister. she knew if she played and socialized with them eventually she would find out. You wouldn't so happen to know a guy by the name of Niko, would you? I think that's where I see you at, I'm one of his clients. OH NO, that must've been my sister, some people do say we favor, but that's her husband. Oh, okay yes, I was trying to figure it out. I said to myself as I walked in, this woman looks so familiar. Well yes, I just want a room for tonight. handing Viola her room key. I'm Jessica by the way, enjoy your stay with us tonight. Hi Jessica and thanks for assisting me. I'm going to leave a key here for my friend. She should be arriving shortly; her name is Simone you can just send her right up.

Thirty minutes later Simone came creeping in. Well that was clever of you, what now? she asked. She gets off at eleven, we are going to hang around in the lobby until she leaves, follow her home, and just whoop her ass. Or is that too dramatic Viola asked.

She is not our victim, his wife is. Simone added yes, but if we beat her ass we can damage her house leave a note, eventually she will call the cops and her sister I'm sure. BOOM! her sister comes rushing to the rescue. Boom! she finds the note, sees the damage, or better yet we steak out there until she comes, follow her home whoop her ass then whatever happens from there I would have to figure it out because that's all I got.

Simone and Viola fell back on the bed in laughed insanely hard until their stomachs started to ache. This reminds me of back in the day when we used to fight everyday all day. I don't want to go back to the old me but this bitch has to get dealt with, fucking up my expensive shit. I worked my ass off for the things I have. I'm not going to let a bitter sick wife destroy shit of mine. I have to at least get to the bottom of everything before things unfold and gets too out of hand.

Well don't you think if we were to get caught "god forbid we do" but if we were too how much more of a disaster things will be. Yeah I feel you Simone but something has to be done and fast.

I don't want anything ruining my lifestyle or my reputation. I care more about that than my marriage, sad to say but hell its plenty more men of status who would love to have me.

Simone laughed, you are a mess. But let's plan this out thoroughly, that way we won't have to worry about anything. Not a finger print, not a spot of our blood. I still have the stuff we got from the convenience store that day...

Eleven o'clock came quickly. As the girls rushed to the car trying to keep a low profile dressed in all black. Simone complained the whole time, due to the fact it was scorching hot out.

Pull around back so she wouldn't notice us. Viola said "Even if she did notice us who would think we were up to something. Everything about us is innocent."

Simone and Viola hid out on the side of the hotel until they seen Jessica walk out.

Simone grabbed the tape and rope from out the backseat as she unraveled it laughing to herself, she felt as if she was on how to get away with murder. Simone put that goddamn rope back where you got it, we are not about to kill nobody. Viola yelled at her.

Like come on she's pulling out, put on your serious face. As if I'm serious we've been laughing and giggling all night. I don't even think I'm mad about it anymore. Simone turned on some old get crunk music so she could get back in a don't give a fuck mood.

Viola we've thought about everything except how we were going to get into her house once we got there.

I already got that together. If we're going to be savages about this we are going to ambush her in the house. I have my gun, I got my black wig. Here paint on you some black thick eyebrows so you won't look noticeable, handing Simone a black thick eyeliner. What if someone's home, Simone asked!!

Stop asking twenty-one questions fifty cent, we are doing this tonight. There's no turning back now. We've got shit to do tomorrow so let's handle this and get back to work. We gone make it out alive safe and unnoticeable so let's not fuck this up. As they turned onto Philip Street Jessica slowly pulled into her driveway to stop an get the mail which set by the curb in front of her house. That gave them amply amount of time to park, jump out the car and rush towards her door. Women always takes twenty minutes to get out the car, we should be able to get to her bushes si-lently. Peeking at Simone, Viola had to make sure she was comprehending correctly. As soon as she unlocks the door I'm going to pull the gun out to aIm it at the back of her head while you push her into the door. Luckily the lights were off at her crib so no one was there. Are you ready? Simone nodded to agree.

As Jessica walked towards her door and rambled for her key. Viola jumped out the bushes, cocking the gun directly at her neck. OPEN THE DOOR QUICKLY BITCH!

Jessica screamed in shock, raising her hands as if she was being arrested. No put your hands down and open the door, shaking in complete fright trying to keep calm. As she opened the door Simone shoved her to the ground. Viola pulled the draw-string of her hoody tighter to disguise herself properly. Simone kicked her in the back of her head multiple of times to make sure she wouldn't turn to recognize them. As Viola knocked down all her pictures and wall frames, she poured bleach all around the kitchen counters and ran water to over flow the kitchen. Viola took some lawn scissors she seen place in the pantry and cut up her fluffy white furniture. She wanted to make sure she destroyed every single item in her house so her sister can feel the same pain she felt when she seen how damaged her crib was. Viola got carried away with destroying her things. She almost forgot that this wasn't her vic-tim. Realizing that she whispered to Simone "come on, let's go!" They both grabbed the girl and shoved her into the hallway closet. Trying to catch her breath inhaling, exhaling, and fighting for her life she finally gave up laying her body towards the back wall of the closet. Viola and Simone cut the lights off and ran full speed down the block, jumped into their vehicle and sped off.

Wow this has to be the sickest shit we've ever done. Simone said to Viola in a nerv-ous tone while checking her surroundings making sure the police or nosey neighbors didn't catch what was going on. But around that time, they were long gone and back to the other side of town.

So much fuel had been in the air with Miya and Simone every time we came together to discuss and plan the wedding the both argued. Even though I knew why Simone was mad, I was still tired of it all. Hell, it was my day everything was supposed to be about me. I couldn't take the shit anymore. Simone had been seeing Darius every night and day. In which it showed on Miya's face that everything hasn't been good at home. She wasn't as happy as she was when she first met him, and for some odd reason I felt bad and the one responsible for it all. My life was filled with so much drama that I couldn't bare too much more of and just when I thought I solved one problem here comes another one.

CHAPTER 8

Babe let's take a break from the world. I got us a few hours at Jacuzzi suites. We need some us time Miya said talking to Darius from out the bathroom. Tonight, we can leave around nine.

Darius wasn't too excited about the plans Miya had for them. I'm tired! I've had a long day let alone week. Don't you think I know that, stepping out of the tub with bubble suds still dripping from her leg. I wanted us to have some alone time without our phones giving us a chance to relax. Miya said as she wrapped her right arm around his shoulder. I'm leaving town this weekend for a business trip and right now I just need your warmth and touch. The thought of you inside me while I'm gone will be hectic for me. I also know you're stressed out about a lot. I just want to take care of you, leaning in closer to feel Darius body heat. He gently moved her arms from around him while reaching for his liquor he had left over from the other night. I'm not in the mood.

Miya felt a standoffish vibe from Darius she felt him slowly fading away from her grasp. The moment she thought she had him wrapped around her finger he was start-ing to show her otherwise and at this point it was too late she had already fell in love.

Following Darius into the kitchen yelling, what the fuck is it? Is it someone else? So, do you not find me attractive any more, Miya asked questions after questions as Darius stared at her so uninterested taking another sip of his drink. He completely ignored every question Miya had asked him. Sitting there reminiscing about Simone all night he grabbed his keys and stormed out the front door.

Miya watched the door for about twenty minutes hoping he would returned but he never came back in. Talking to herself, I could make things better but if it's another woman I'm already too late. Stepping back into her oval tub where the bubbles had already dissolved, she sunk her body in deeply and just exhaled. After an hour of soaking and wrecking her brain Miya realized she needed advice calling Viola she always has the answers.

Viola picked up sounding tired on the count of it being 3 am in the morning. I'm sorry to call you this late but my mind won't let me rest. It's so much confusion going on. The moment I finally decide to fall in love with someone the moment he starts to act up. I am not a fucking liability I'm an asset. I bring more to the table than pussy, hell I am the fucking table. I mean even though a man with Darius status turns me on and makes my pussy more wet than ever, I'm still that bitch. Right, trying to get Viola to feel her! Yes, you are right, Viola agreed just to get her to shut the hell up.

I'm losing my mojo meanwhile I can have any guy I want in Springfield. There's never a shortage when it comes to men, but it's just something about his sexy dark ass. Miya rambled on and on before she felt that Viola was no longer listening' she was sound asleep. Miya finally hung up.

Days passed and it was almost time for Miya to leave state. Still haven't heard from Darius since he stormed out the house the other night. It was time for her to head to the airport so she decided to reach out to him before she left. After calling him continuously, still no answer. I'll just make a stop by his crib Miya said as she locked her doors and grabbed her suitcases, pulling up to the gated community so hesitant to enter. She had the code to the gate when everything was perfect with the two of them. She pressed the code and soon the gate opened, she fixed her blouse and lip-stick as she pulled into the driveway. Spotting a red Dior bag on the table through the window, Miya's heart dropped. She couldn't believe who she was staring at, laying across the couch in some silky pajamas eating Breakfast and sipping on a mimosa. It was Simone! Darius laid back on the couch with a tray of grapes, laughing and cuddling with her. Miya leaned her head closer toward the window so she could peep in on the conversation they were having. Tip toing back into her vehicle she rushed to start her car and pulled off. So mortified and devastated not knowing what to do. She didn't want to be late for her flight so she turned on some groove kind of music and did eighty mph all the way to the airport.

That conniving son of a bitch, I knew something was up. I mean I didn't think it would be something so backstabbing as this. But it was always so much tension between us, I just thought maybe we didn't like the same things, I never would've guessed this bitch would be fucking my man. I wonder why Viola didn't have so much to say about my rants with Darius. She knew all about their sneaky situation. That's her best friend she wouldn't tell on her, but at the same time she wouldn't do me like this neither. Miya cried to herself as she carried her bags to check in. I got to figure some shit out. Texting Viola, call me later this is very urgent, boarding the plane and taking her seat. She closed her eyes and just cried silently asleep.

New York, New York!!

Meetings after meetings today so hectic but enticingly good, I got my contracts signed to open business here in downtown New York. Everything hasn't been so good with my relationship life. I've been betrayed by a so call friend. But god is awesome. Miya packed her briefcase up and headed to Starbucks for an ice cappuc-cino. Even though it was a bit nippy out Miya couldn't go a day without her ice cap.

Sitting in a star bucks filled with many business savvy people with open laptops, Miya double looked at a familiar face hiding in the back corner. As she got up and walked toward their direction, she dropped her drink all over the floor. The whole establishment starred at her, but she wasn't embarrassed at all. She couldn't believe what she was seeing, it was Elizabeth. Hiding behind a couple of newspapers, in which Liz had already seen Miya the moment she walked in. Miya has always been the nosey type she had a wondering eye. She peeped and watched everything. She could really catch a thief in the night.

Liz Look at you!!! How are you? leaning forward to give her a hug. Liz body tem-perature had to be over the normal temp. With quivers and shyness, Liz kept looking away from Miya.

Is everything okay? Do you need help, where have you been, I'm so happy to see you? Liz kept glancing away not wanting her to directly talk to her.

With cigarette burns in her shirt, holes at the side of her shoe, and a shaved head Miya could barely recognize her. Her eyes were blood shot red with scratches covering every piece of her face.

Liz, its Miya! Your friend, I have been reaching out to you for the longest. We have been worried sick about you. Yes, I'm fine, shaking and taking another sip of her coffee ordering the cashier to bring her more crèmes. I have a new number.

What are you doing out here, do you need some money, is everything okay. Come home! Miya said to Liz.

Everything is fine, how are my girls? Tell them mommy loves and miss them. Liz pulled a picture out of a ripped used Burberry wallet. As she kissed the picture, can you bring them to me. All I want to see is my girls. How is Harlem? I haven't heard from him in months. The bastard doesn't check up on me anymore.

As tears started to fall from Miya's eyes, she realized Liz had been smoking crack. She spotted a tube of cocaine on the side of the table. Liz has turned into a complete crackhead in just a few months.

Liz Harlem is dead. You killed him

I killed him!! I did no such things; I would never kill my husband I love that man. If he's dead who has my girls scratching her arm intensively.

Miya completely ignored her question.

Grabbing Liz so she could get down to what was really going on with her, wiping her tears as they walked out the door.

Why would you just up and leave like that Liz. You are a mess a complete wreck. Liz ignored Miya for as long as she could. She patted herself down, searching for her tube of drugs. Getting very angry, Miya what's up? You are so pretty you have always been beautiful and always had it going on. Sobbing and dragging her voice, Miya didn't want to cry anymore listening to how tore up Liz had become.

Which was so unlike her to get like this, she barely even got drunk.

I always wanted to be like you, you and Viola stayed on top. I mean I remembered I had it going on, but hell it wasn't my shit. I was just a house wife. Harlem paid for everything, but I still had bitches all over jealous of me. I stayed laced and strapped up with dolce and Dior bags. These bitches still not fucking with me, Miya stared at Liz so astonished. She listened even though Liz obviously haven't checked a mirror or seen a dentist in a minute.

Liz had to remember her circumstance she didn't want to scare her into running off. She pretended as if she was okay with the awkward situation they were in. Even though she wanted to remind her she had killed her husband, she didn't want to seem so blunt. Maybe she's playing with my head she knows we all know she killed her husband. I mean I don't know too much about crack but I know a muthafucka will remember if they killed somebody or not. Let's face it, she was out of her mind and there was no getting her back.

What's been going on with you? Liz asked.

I've been great. I'm out here for business, I found the man of my dreams, well I thought I did. Viola and Simone backstabbed me without a care in the world. The minute I thought I found true love here goes my wake-up call. I never thought for a second I would have to second guess my friend, but ever since Simone moved to Springfield's Viola been acting different. It's something about her that she's hiding, I just don't know yet.

Everybody isn't who they say they are. Liz said

Turning her head in the opposite direction'

What does that supposed to mean? Miya asked. Nothing let's just change the subject, enough about those two. Scratching insanely, Liz started to Fein for more drugs, which had left Miya uncertain because she didn't know how to supply her with the drugs she needed. She told Liz she could stay the night at her hotel so she wouldn't be on the streets. Even though Liz had turned herself into a complete crack head she still couldn't leave her on the streets like that. Liz was still her friend and she still cared about her more than ever. Wishing Viola would have never played her the way she did, the anticipation on calling her was real. She wanted to share the news of her seeing Liz and what she had become. It was a happy but devastating feeling to see her girl go from living so abundantly to barely remembering who she was. Just the thought of Liz's situation made her teary.

Miya knew after that night she probably wouldn't ever see Liz again. After hours trying to help her find a decent place the only thing Liz wanted was money for crack. She didn't cooperate with anything Miya was trying to do for her.

Later that night Miya sat outside of her hotel balcony and thought about how awful her friends had betrayed her. She didn't want to spaze out or confront them about anything. She felt the need to do something very revengeful and spiteful. Something that will ruin the both of them, she wanted to fuck up their life and get them to feel the pain she was feeling when she seen her man with Simone. Miya knew she didn't have anything on neither of them. Her first thought was to fuck Trey. Realizing she would have to go out her way to get Trey to even consider she knew that was too much. She thought to make up a big lie about Viola and spread it secretly so it would get back to Trey. But that was too Immature. Walking out on the balcony, Liz had joined Miya, with powder across her nose Miya couldn't stand to see it.

What's up Miya, is you okay? Miya was tired of holding everything back, she sat Liz down and shared with her everything that was going on. She knew Liz wasn't going to run back and tell anyone anything. But at this point Miya didn't give a shit. As she told Liz how foul Simone and Viola had done her. Liz took another sniff of her drugs and concluded on with her response.

Let me tell you like this Liz said as she scooted two pillows between her feet. When you think you have everything figured out? When life is so perfect for you, you feel like god has blessed you exceedingly. You feel like you're the luckiest lady in the world. You start to feel so confident about yourself to the point some days you don't wear makeup or get dressed up because you're that happy. The minute you think your fairytale fantasies had become your reality. Life hits you, and when life hits you it hits you hard. Look at me, this is life hitting me. This is me not ever knowing who I was. I was a stay at home mom. I was married with two beautiful children. I had everything I wanted plus more. I thought I was secure and safe. I thought I had friends that would never betray or disrespect me. I thought my husband was the jay to my Z. I thought you guys loved me. That life was so perfect that I forgot who I was. I lost myself. After finding out about Harlem's affairs with women, and seeing how he had more than enough mistresses. He had two other children by two other women. I lost my mind. Seeing that my best friend wasn't who she said she was. I believed in her, I consoled in her. I told her all my problems and she gave me the greatest advice. I thought so highly of her until one day I find out she's a full-blown prostitute.

As Liz proceeded on, Miya eyes widen in disbelief! She would have never guessed that. Trying to figure out if Liz was just high and didn't know what she was talking about. She figured she would say anything. But Liz was kind of making sense, eve-rything she had said about Viola added up. We never been to her job she never talked about anything in that nature. Even though I saw her with a group of girls before, knowing now how slick Viola was she probably rented a group of girls just to dis-guise her filthy lifestyle. I needed more details though. I needed to know more about this situation. Liz went on and on about Harlem and Viola as Miya tuned her out. I mean at this point no one is talking about the death of Harlem anymore. And no one cares about the absence of Liz. This is a juicy headline. If I talked to Liz more about the tea she had on

Viola and how she knew Viola was a trick. That could be my revenge. It was on at this point and I knew exactly how to get back at them.

There's no place like home.

It was horrible seeing a good friend ruin her life that, within a blink of an eye. The news with Liz was so juicy I wanted to tell Viola. I couldn't see myself talking or even hanging with her again though knowing how bad she betrayed me. Me talking to her would ruin my revenge against her. They think they're shady, well shady is my middle name. All I had to do was stick around them a little longer, find more juice on Viola and her life would be ruined. Evil laughs came from Miya as she planned to sabotage Viola.

Viola had to meet up with her bridesmaids to go over rehearsal and to meet the grooms. Miya wasn't too excited to see none of them not even Darius. In fact, she hasn't spoken to him since she came back from New York. I'm sure he's been out with Simone anyway she thought to herself as she pulled up to the location. It's going to be very awkward trying to pretend as if she didn't know about Darius and Simone. Just the thought of it made her even more excited to destroy her life.

Viola arrived twenty minutes late due to springs fields horrible traffic. she had to make a detour to pick up Mona, Simones friend from high school. She had reached out to her because she needed another bridesmaid due to Liz's absence. Simone was happy to see Mona even though she barely recognized her. She had gotten so fat. Viola was so private she forgot to mention seeing her when she first moved to Springfield. As the girls chatted and rehearsed. Mild tension in the room started to develop with Miya and Simone. It was no secret at this point, everyone knew they hated each other. Viola loudly interrupted them both when Trey and Darius entered the room. She knew what was going on. Still not having the urge to tell her fiancé without seeming messy. She thought to keep it to herself and just act surprise if things hit the air. Darius stepped into formation without acknowledging either Simone or Miya. Everything was so confusing and uncomfortable and only a handful of them really knew the real reason. Mona realized that this supposed to be happy day wasn't so pleasant. As she seen Miya walk into the women's restroom, she fol-lowed her. By the time she entered Miya was already in a stall, Mona searched through her bag to grab her phone. She conversed with someone who seemed to have asked her a million and one questions. Exiting the bathroom stall preparing to wash her hands. Miya stared into the mirror seeing it was the girl that came in late with viola. Wondering who she was, she properly introduced herself. Trying to figure out where she had come from. She started to ask her general questions.

Where do you know Viola from?

Did you guys meet here in spring field. Miya asked.

No I grew up with her and Simone. We attended high school together which is so awkward I'm here at her wedding. I never was cool enough to hang with them. Miya giggled to herself as Mona proceeded along with her stories. Miya knew right then she had a gullible flunky that she could befriend and help her. What else do you know about her besides the fact she was a bully back in high school. Miya asked. Well that's about it, she seems a bit different now.

Of course, she's different now. It's been years, usually people grow up after high school. I mean it don't always mean their ways change if you know what I mean. Grinning and winking an eye at Mona. Mona was so in the dark she didn't have a clue of what Miya was hinting at.

This should be a wonderful wedding, she has a very amazing and supportive fiancé. Mona said.

People are breaking up more than getting together, this is a major fucking deal. I can't wait until my big day. Miya looked at Mona wondering why she was so damn lost and dingy. I know for a fact Viola never hung with her in High school. She's way to cool for her. She thought to herself as they walked back into the banquet room for rehearsals.

I can't let this wedding go on. Something has to take place within the next week before this wedding. These hoes got me fucked up if they think they're getting away with backstabbing me. That's when it clicked. Miya had the perfect solution on how she was going to sabotage Viola. Right after rehearsals she rushed to her car and drove off.

Let's get down to business. It was a week from violas wedding and she still was on bullshit. Viola knew she had to make sure her bank account had at least half of million in it before she got married. Hell wasn't no way in hell I was sitting in the house with my hand out waiting on a man to give me money for nails and hair. Viola thought to herself. I don't see how females are content with being lazy like that. I was born around all hustlers, shit plus my pops would kill me if he seen me wanting anything from a man. He always told me I was his way out the hood. Meanwhile I listened to my mother first and went to college. She didn't want me to be dependent either but she wanted me to take the longer route. I listened for a year but that shit got played out quick. My dad was right, I have what it takes to be my own boss and to make millions. I was determined to take care of my family and that's what I did.

CHAPTER 9

It was almost time to get fitted for my dress when I got an unexpected text from Niko. My first thought was to ignore it because it could've been his loco wife pretending to be him. These fuckers just didn't get it, yet still wondering what was it he wanted. Last time I talked to him he went off on me which was quite satisfying because I thought I got rid of him. Granted, I knew I didn't need any more money because I was financially stable at this point in my life. But for some odd reason, I wanted to text back. Even though his wife had totally damaged my crib. It was some-thing about him that I liked. I think I kind of got used to him popping in and out of my life on bullshit. Snapping back into reality, I was a week away from being a bride. My entire family will be here watching me walk down the aisle. But, I still didn't know if I was in love or not. Something felt out of place, I couldn't exactly put my finger on the issue. But for some random reason I get this feeling that some-thing is happening behind my back. Calling Simone making sure she was okay while they measured my waist and boobs. Where are you? Viola asked, are you okay? Yes, Simone replied I'm fine! What's wrong?

Just checking on you. Are you with Darius? No, I'm done with Darius. I'm out mak-ing money ill hit you back in a minute. As Simone hung up the phone, and unknown number dialed in. Viola was in no mood to play with no one today so she ignored the call.

Just a couple of days before the wedding and Trey was super nervous. He walked into his own bachelor party which looked like a parade. His teammates made sure this night was one to remember. The room was filled with strippers and models walking around with nothing but gold bows covering their nipples and vagina. As Treys eyes widen he realize this was going to be the last night as a free man. Why not enjoy it he said as he sat down and got a lap dance from a light skin chick with big boobs. Suddenly a knock on the door, in which everyone ignored it but Trey, nervously getting up thinking it could've been his soon to be wife. As he got up to open the door he seen no one was there. Closing the door, thinking someone was probably surprising him with more dancers or something. He seen a small brown package wrapped in duck-tape. Grabbing the box as he slowly took a step back to shut the door. Trey placed the box on the counter and went back to enjoy his table dance. A few hours later as everyone was leaving, Darius and another teammate stayed after to help clean up. Darius grabbed the brown box asking Trey where did he want it placed. Somebody dropped that off earlier, I forgot to open it. I wonder whose it from. Trey said as he ripped the box open.

Standing there, flabbergasted Trey couldn't believe what his eyes was seeing.

What's in the box? A couple of teammates asked as Trey fell back into the chair. Trey was furious and stuck. He didn't know what to say or how to react. He stared at the box so long until his eyes watered.

Trey come on, what's wrong with you? What's in the box. Darius yelled.

Trey finally handed the frame over to his teammates so embarrassed and devastated. Grabbing his keys and phone, he stormed out of his home.

A few hours later, viola pranced in the house, looking around seeing no one was there. She knew it was his bachelor party night but didn't see a car in the driveway. Hmm, that's weird. I wonder where everyone is. Probably at a strip club, she thought to herself as she grabbed her phone to call Trey.

Calling him repeatedly with no answer.

Viola didn't think anything of it, assuming he was somewhere super intoxicated.

The next morning viola woke up too many missed calls but none from Trey. Before she dialed him, she hit Simone back seeing she had called her over ten times.

Bitch why haven't you been answering your phone? I was sleep, what's wrong. Vi-ola asked as she sat on the edge of the bed. Trey is calling off the wedding. Darius texted me late last night drunk as hell wanting to come over and spilled the beans to me. He told me a package was delivered to his house during his bachelor party while all his teammates were there. It was pictures of you and some man butt ass naked. He didn't really get into too much detail, in which he didn't have to because I already knew what that was about. I tried calling you but you didn't answer. Viola stomach had fell right to her feet. She felt like a ton of bricks had crushed her heart. That's why he hadn't been returning my calls. Viola dropped her head. What am I going to do? The wedding is in two days. I don't know how I'm going to fix things in 48 hours. Everyone will be here in the morning, and I just don't… ill be over in thirty minutes, Simone interrupted viola and hung up.

Viola had been calling Trey all day. At that point, she knew the reason behind eve-rything. He hadn't come home or nothing. I can only Imagine the things he's saying about me. I can hear his friends in his ear telling him "you can't turn no hoe into a housewife"! I mean I could lie about the whole thing on the count of I haven't been in the city long enough to say the photos were old. Shaking her head in disbelief. He will never believe me. I should just skip town. Maybe I should kill him and go hide out like Liz. Hell, I know one of these days I got to face everyone and tell them the truth. I know Trey will not show up. I wonder where he's at.

I thought all of this was over, I wonder was that the reason Niko was calling my phone the other night. His wife probably put him out. I got to meet with him. His wife was right when she said to never mess with a married man. She's trying her best to ruin me.

Viola pondered calling Trey numerous of times knowing he wasn't going to pick up. She reached out to Niko as well, no one answered for her. Ninety-nine problems and all these niggas are one Viola rapped out loud. I can't believe I'm going through this shit. This isn't my life; this shit is for the birds. Trey know he is dead wrong for treating me like some step child. He knew I was a freak when I sucked his dick from the back. I don't know why he's acting brand-new like this pussy not good enough to sell. That would be the death of him though, finding out my real hustle. Fuck those pictures, those could be burned and buried. To know I probably made more than him in one month than he does in six would kill him softly.

Trying to put all clues together to how and why somebody would try to ruin me like this. I came up with nothing. The only person I could think of was Niko wife. How-ever, I didn't know this woman from a can of paint. It just couldn't be her. Viola jumped into her car and went to a nearby pharmacy.

Twenty-Four hours until the wedding and the only message I receive from Trey was him asking for the keys back to my brand-new range rover. He can be mad all day and tomorrow, but wasn't no way I was giving those keys back. How selfish of him to not at least reach out and see what was going on. I knew exactly where he would be around this time, yet still unlucky because my mom and dad had landed and I had to meet them within the next hour. Which is crazy, my parents had never met Trey. I told them so much about him but with everything happening so fast I don't think they'll ever meet him. Everyone was so excited to see me. More cousins from back home had flown out and I just didn't have it in me to tell them the bad news. What a fucking inconvenience for them. Soon I was going to have to them but still haven't gotten in touch with Trey. I mean at least we could talk about it and tell them together. My mom didn't have a clue of what I did for money out here, so I had to prepare myself for the big talk with her and pops. I been out here in Spring-field for months, I'm sure we have a lot to catch up on. Let them tell it, me on the other hand don't want to catch up on anything. I'm going to lie about everything anyway.

Pulling up to the airport, my parents was so excited to see me. The smile on my mother's face was to die for. Which reminded me of the reasons I went so hard, just to see that smile right there.

Hey ma, hey pops.

Hugs and kisses from the both of them.

My mom didn't waste any time on the questions. So, where is he? I can't wait to meet my son in law. Mom said as she threw her suitcase on my expensive leather. Her and Simone just didn't have any respect for expensive things. I haven't talked to him today, I'm sure he's somewhere super nervous. The big day is tomorrow. Isn't that how men are?

He better not had gotten cold feet after we just flew this long way. Dad interrupted. I got to talk to this new son in law of mine. Where are we staying, my back hurt and I'm starving.

Dad was always grouchy after a long day of anything. He didn't play about his food, newspaper, or daughter. I can only Imagine the things he would say to Trey after I tell him Trey was calling the wedding off.

Dad was always on my side no matter what I did or how wrong I was. I was always his little princess in his eyes I could do no wrong. I still didn't want to keep it that real with him and tell him about anything just yet. I honestly didn't have a clue to what I was going to do. Luckily, I still had my place they could stay at while I figured things out. Which is another problem I had, I always think I can figure things out when I wanted too. The wedding was in twenty-four hours and I still haven't talked to my fiancé.

Arriving at the church, it was super early. I couldn't believe how beautiful the wedding planners had decorated the venue. White centifolia roses were everywhere fill-ing up the entire aisle. Crystal waterfalls with Mr. and Mrs. Furgerson falling from it made my dream wedding come to reality. I sat at the alter hoping Trey would walk in for a last-minute rehearsal. Still no one in sight. I called him a few more times before getting the point that he didn't want anything to do with me. I should just call everyone and let them know what was going on. My other thoughts were telling me to just proceed on with the wedding and if he didn't show up to look at it as if he had experience cold feet. By this time, it was going on ten and all my bridesmaids was pulling up.

Hey Simone, have you talked to Darius. Viola asked as Simone walked through the double doors of the church. The last time I talked to him was last night and he told me wasn't no way Trey was coming. I tried to get more information from him but he said he wasn't coming neither. Trey said he wasn't marrying a slut. I'm guessing more information had gotten back to him.

Seconds later as the two were conversing, everyone started to walk in. All my brides-maid was looking remarkably beautiful. I was very astonished at the way the deco-rators had three human angels hanging very stiffly from the thick ropes. Meanwhile still trying to figure out my plans I tiptoed into my dressing room looked out the curtains, more guest had arrived.

A firm knock tapped on the door. I was hesitant to get up an answer it. I let them knock until they went away. A thin envelope slid up under the door, as I leaned towards the floor to grab it. I seen a red lipstick print on the back of it. As I slowly opened the envelope I read the bottom of the letter first which said love Elizabeth. My heart started to beat fast because lord knows I missed Liz and today was my wedding day and she wasn't present. As I read the letter she told me news that I would have never in a million years expected.

"Dear Viola, its Liz. I know what you're thinking where am I and how do I know where you are. I don't want to bore you and tell you about my problems and where-abouts, just know I'm hanging in there. I've recently met with Miya. She told me you were a snake for hooking your girlfriend up with her man. The thought of know-ing you could have possibly slept with my husband made me engaged into the con-versation more. But Isn't that how life works these days, Every man for themselves huh? Anything for a check? We both know I know about you, in which I was never going to speak to you again because of it. But hell, still I wanted you to know to watch your back. I'm probably sounding like a snake myself but hey, I have nothing to lose. She told me you were getting married and I found the address on an invitation tucked in her suitcase. You may never see or hear from me again so take care of yourself. Don't end up like me"

Miya was my girl so I thought, and even though Simone warned me about her her whole reason for being my friend was to destroy me over some dude she barely knew. It just didn't add up though. I hooked up with Niko way before Simone started to date Darius. It couldn't have been her wrecking my home and sending me threats. I mean at this point I didn't know who to trust. Everything was falling out of place at once and so unexpectedly. I knew Miya would be pulling up soon if she wasn't already here. I texted Simone to tell her the news I just received. In which she didn't waste any time coming to my room.

I told you she was a snake, Simone said as she read the letter. Who even sent you this letter?

That don't even matter Simone. What am I going to do now? I got a whole bunch of snakes around me that thinks I'm a snake. Trey isn't coming to his own wedding. Miya found out about you and Darius so there's no telling what she's up to. She hasn't said two words to me about it, so I know she's contemplating something. As viola ranted on about her problems Simone fixed the curls that had fell from her pasting back and forth. Listen viola, everyone thinks they got your back against the wall. What you have to do is stay two steps ahead of anyone that think they can out smart you. You have to remember who you are and where you come from. If they want to play, play back. You are in control of your own problems. Fix them before they break you.

Viola wrapped her just married robe around her body as she agreed to what Simone was telling her. You right, I'm going to go out there and let everyone know the weeding is cancelled. And I'm going to handle this shit.

Miya walked in the door with a smile and some congratulations cards from a few guests. Cut the shit Miya, Viola snapped at her with no hesitation. She was tired of playing with bitches at this point. What are you trying to do? We know you know about Simone and Darius. We are all grown, you and her can hash it out like women and never speak again for all I give a shit. Miya had no clue this was coming, she had plans on her finding out she knew another and better way. Trying to figure out how she knew. Viola never mentioned the letter from Liz. So, what was your plans huh? Simone added. Were you trying to destroy her wedding? Me and Darius are in love and I don't like you. As a matter a fact I never liked you. He doesn't like you. Yelling so loud trying to reach at her. Viola jumped in between them both trying to break up the argument. But they were both so amped it was Impossible to calm them down. So much rage and aggravation came from them both which brought a lot of attention to their dressing room. Violas mom quickly rushed in. What's all the loud fussing and cursing about? As other bridesmaids and family members of viola en-tered the room.

Viola tried to calm the chaos in the room down. Meanwhile trying to separate from it all. Running towards the kitchen to hide out. She couldn't help but notice usb cords attached to a video recorder connecting from a projector that led to the church which was placed behind the alter. As she grabbed one of the cameras she seen a box below with her and Nikos naked pictures. Her whole faced fell to the floor as she fumbled with the camera. I can't believe Miya was trying to take me out like this. This is pass the normal retaliation; this bitch is deranged. I mean what if the wedding was still on. The time was set for three pm to start playing. I would've been so uncomfortable and ashamed. Lord knows!

CHAPTER 10

Wedding bells...

The church was soon surrounded by paparazzi, news reporters, fans, and camera men, all scattered around and through the church. Treys family was seated on his side of the room and viola side on the opposite. Viola felt like a dog with her head cut off running around trying to figure her next move out. Two hours had passed and she still was clueless. Seeing Treys car pull up behind a dumpster that was parked in the back of the church. Her heart raced as if she seen a ghost. She fled to the back to approach him, when his only mission was to come and call off the wedding. Why are you doing this to me? Viola whispered. Trey ignored her as he lightly pushed her shoulder away from his sight. I don't have anything to say to you. I want to kindly apologize to my family and friends for the inconvenience. I spent thousands of dollars trying to make sure this wedding was the best day of your life. To only find out my soon to be wife tricks for a living. Trey I can explain, viola shouted out. There's no need to do that, you don't owe me an explanation for living a foul life. I've seen it all, and for some reason I feel like you were trying to tell me this all along. I just didn't pay attention to the signs.

What signs Trey? The sticky notes left on my seat and car windows. The pornos I found on the backseat of your car. The open condoms I seen in your bathroom trash. The room keys to Fantasy stay you dropped in my driveway. I just didn't want to believe it. I guess love is blind.

Viola ran back towards the dressing room. Looking for Miya, in which she was no-where in sight. She rushed towards the front of the church barefoot looking as if someone had robbed her. Cameras started to flash as she turned around and over-looked her peers. The thought of wanting to pound Miya's face in, she cared about nothing else but that. This whole time she thought Nikos wife was the one behind all this madness. Looking to her left she seen Miya stepping into her car. Viola didn't think twice about the paparazzi and fans standing around waiting to see the big wedding. She charged in the direction of her vehicle, balling up her left fist swinging it at the back of her head. The alarm went off Immediately causing everyone to look in that direction, seeing Viola and her bridesmaid scuffle back and forth. Miya driver seat was slightly cracked as she had already fell to the ground, trying to grab her pocket knife out to protect her face. Viola had already gotten the best of her, beating her face insanely into the ground with no mercy or spare of her cry for help. Viola was fed up and mentally tired of all the bullshit that had been happening around her. As cameras and news reporters gathered around, no one broke It up. Treys family and friends had heard the chaos as they ran outside to see what was going on. Miya and Viola was already handcuffed at that time. Violas parents rushed out screaming and crying. What's going on? It's my daughter's wedding day, let her out of those handcuffs. Viola what did you do wrong, why is there a knife in your hand? Her mom started to panic. Simone charged towards the police officer so amped and mad she missed the broad. She went towards Miya and coughed up a full mouth of spit splashing it all over her right cheekbone. Another officer had grabbed Simone and handcuffed her also. While friends, fans and family stood there flabbergasted and at a loss of words. Trey was completely humiliated and embarrassed. He didn't know what to do or say to the officers or the reporters in which they were recording live on the channel four news.

By the time anyone could defend themselves to the officers for their surrender, more police cars had arrived. Loud sirens and k9 dogs had the church seeming like it was a Friday night at club Med. Viola stared the other way seeing more cameras flashing in Treys direction. She knew he was beyond furious, the frustration on his face and the sweat rolling from his forehead said it all and she knew it was all her fault.

One officer walked up waving his badge looking like Samuel L Jackson. Tall, thick mustache, shirt fitted his chest like a glove with an extensive tone. He took his job super serious standing in the center trying to clear out the crowd. As another stepped in front of him, waving a sheet of paper trying to get everyone's attention. Trey stared at me as if he was plotting to kill me next. I told him I would never embarrass him and I did just that.

Simone Owens & Viola Williams one officer yelled out. As I lifted my head back up, Simone stared at me in complete fright. We both were confused to how they knew our name. In the back of my mind, I thought Miya had did some more malicious shit to demolish me. Which made me once again not regret the ass whopping I just gave her. But worst, A lady with a black suit and baby kitten heels walked up behind them approaching us both. Knowing exactly who was who, signaling a warrant out on behalf of a woman by the name of Jessica Simmons.

Scared straight. I didn't know if it was karma coming around quicker than usual or if I was just being betrayed by a bunch of sensitive pussies.

Trying to catch eye contact with Simone to make sure we were on the same page. We been through shit like this before as kids. In and out of police cars and jail, so we both knew the rules to not say anything without a lawyer present or hell just play dumb until both were free. Either way it goes we both knew not to tell on one another, so I wasn't really worried about that. I gave her the "it's time" look. Even though at this point I couldn't really trust anyone. My dad was behind my shoulder on the phone with some city friends trying to pull a few strings as if they would have any connections with the system in Springfield. My mom wouldn't stop crying, I wanted to yell shut the fuck up so bad. Meanwhile having to walk pass Treys entourage and family was the most embarrassing thing ever. I leaned my down and got in the back of the police car.

I lifted my hand placing it on the window, saying my goodbyes to Trey and parents. He turned his back on me and walked away. They had placed me and Simone in the same cell. Fucking goofballs, knowing we were going to figure out a way to get out of here. She was still super solid to me, even though I wasn't putting anything behind my own damn mother at this point. They watched us talk for a few moments. An officer opened the bars on the cell to take Simone into a sound proof room. He had to be questioning her for about three hours because I had fallen asleep, waking up to the door of the room wide open. I figured they took her into her own cell. The kitten heel lady passed my cell winking at me. I didn't know what the wink was all about until she stepped backwards to tell me I had court at eight a.m. and to have my shit together. I always hated women like her. She was stuck sitting at an office desk all day trying to be super save a hoe that she thinks innocent. Like come on now ma, you look miserable. You should come work for me. Joking to myself, knowing I was about to beat this case because I knew they didn't have anything on me. As I sat and pondered my thoughts, the only name I could think about that could've said anything to anyone was Simone's friend Joi. I couldn't wait to see her and I knew Simone was thinking the same thing. I don't know how I stepped out of bound anyway. I know better to have flaky bitches around me. I couldn't even look at myself the same way. Hell, if anything I betrayed myself for trusting bitches. Here I am involved with four different situations, in fucking court sitting in a jumpsuit looking like Martha Stewart. Once I seen Simone come out I felt a little less nervous, they sat her on the opposite side of me. My parents were seated behind me. With a few lawyers in at-tendance for us both. There was no way I wasn't going to have anyone represent my homegirl. We had this shit in the bag. The judge was a fat Caucasian man who looked like he didn't take any shit from anyone. So, I had to make sure my mouth was pleasant at all time. He didn't waste any time getting to the point. I looked around to try an peep out a familiar face that could've been the reason behind us being in here. But not a face in sight, not even Joi.

I had seen Mona sitting there, at first I thought she was here for the support of me. Since she was my bridesmaid. Until she sat on the stand to testify against us. Lord knows, I didn't have a clue to what she was going to say. I mean what in the hell was she even doing up there with a box in her hand neatly taped. She didn't want to look at me for shit. But the look on her face was very devious and spiteful. I sat back to contemplate. You would've thought the judge and her was screwing around the way they were smiling and grinning.

We have a witness behind the assault of Jessica Simmons. But not only do we have proof of these twos sadly assaulting this young lady. Miss Williams have major skel-etons in her closet. Now this isn't a freak show, the judge jokingly said. But to find the underlying cause of this case we must watch the video. My eyes teared up still not knowing what information they had on me, but as I looked back at my parents I seen the curiousness in their faces that devastated me furthermore. The projector dropped from behind the judge's neck, I scooted my feet together as sweat dripped from my left thigh. Nervously! You would've though Mona was a biology teacher the way she stood in front of the screen sharing information with the entire court room. A prosecutor started to ask her, why are you being so vindictive? What provoked you to share this information with the court? Aren't you a bridesmaid? What are your issues? I was patiently waiting for her to answer as more sweat fell from my face. Before she pressed play on the screen. She stood forward and proceeded.

"I always hated Viola, because she thought she was all that. She was the only one in school with big boobs and good hair. The entire school liked her, I never knew why she was such a mean girl. She picked and played with everyone and they still jocked her. I remember it like yesterday, I had the biggest crush on Jeremy. He played the clarinet for our high school band. I did everything I could to Impress him until one day on valentine's day we had a skating party at the skate fair. I had worn my pink covers so no one could see how old and dingy my skates were. Thinking I'm cute with my slick curly ponytail and my guess outfit I had just got for my birthday a week before. Even though I wasn't as cool as the other freshmen, I was feeling my-self that day. I had all the confidence in the world, I just knew Jeremy was going to recognize me. As I reached for my glow stick I glanced around the skating rink trying to spot Jeremy. I was hoping he was close by somewhere scoping me out. I seen him standing on the back side of the wall with one hand scratching his head and the other one biting on a pickle. To the left of him was all the cool kids, I never hung with them I just always pretended to like them just to feel safe because they were com-plete jerks. They would laugh and joke about you all day, I was too sensitive so I never wanted to be the one with fingers pointed at me. Every single day

I quickly walked pass their lockers trying to make it to my third hour English class.

As I skated slowly towards the back I tried to be smooth with my glow up sticks and pink covers glowing in and out. I slid one leg behind the other smoothly spinning around to skate backwards. When BOOM!!! My whole life had stopped before my eyes. I sat there for a moment to feel around for my glasses. All I could hear was outrageous obnoxious laughs. When I felt my glasses in the touch of my hands, I quickly put them on. I looked around to see everyone staring laughing and pointing cameras and phones at me. I took my skates off ran to the girl's room with both hands covering my eyes crying dreadfully, so embarrassed. Seeing Jeremy in the crowd laughing along killed my mood and confidence. I never wanted to see him or them again. I skipped my English class for the rest of that semester. My mom thought I needed extra credit, tutoring or even summer school because I failed his class that year. Which is one of the reasons I ended up here in Springfield, I didn't get in Georgia state with my previous g.p.a, I had to settle with Illinois tech community school. When I had seen viola at the airport that day, the look on my face was in disgust. That feeling had triggered through my body all over again. I tried to disguise myself but she had already seen me so I did what I used to do in high school and acted like I was happy to see her.

As we caught up, she told me about her auditions and how she was moving here. The itch in my stomach was drastically excited. As I said my goodbyes, I went home and prayed she didn't make the cut. I prayed that everything she touched would ruin. Every food she ate would make her vomit and everything she would do failed. She called my phone a few days later I'm thinking. I was dreading to answer. I ignored the call because the thought of me wanting to pay her back for my high school humiliation was very vigorous. I wanted her life in pieces. I was so ecstatic when she needed me. Even though it's been five years since the incident I still wanted revenge. Period! After I got all the things I needed to destroy her, hoping my planned work. Mona stopped to smile at Viola.

Inspector gadget? yea yea, call me what you want. I decided to return her call. Sure, I'll come get you, Mona said as she pressed play on the remote. You see after I dropped her off, I stalked her every chance I got. From her room stays at eleven o'clock at night, to her daily outings with her friends. I had seen her and simone brutally assault the innocent Miss. Jessica. I had seen her first date with Mr. lover boy. I hotwired her vehicle to insert a hidden camera in the backseat behind the passenger seat. I stayed up day and night for three months watching her every move. I was devoted to my mission and I made sure I succeeded. Her lifestyle was very distasteful, Mona said as she clicked to the next screen. Which made me even more happier. The evidence I had so far was all I really needed but I wanted to be greedy. I wanted to sabotage her whole entire life. From friendships to relationships, so I kept snooping. I pretty much had it in the bag. To see her so unsure of what was going on I laughed every chance I got. Viola didn't have a clue to who was out to get her. I sat in my bed and watched her try to figure it out. From her Hawaii trip to her coming home to a catastrophe. From her late nights sleeping with married men, I took an elevator up to a room above theirs, hid out on a balcony to capture pictures of them both. It was my first time witnessing a pimp pay a trick. To the notes on her car, to the sticky notes and opened condoms I placed in her trash can. I even fiddled and dropped a few hints around Trey so he could catch on. He was so caught up in her ass like everyone else that he didn't have a fucking clue.

The day she asked me to be one of her bridesmaid, I sat there staggered knowing I could end it before it all started. That day at rehearsals, I ducked off to go plant hidden recorders in the church kitchen. I made sure it was set to start playing in the mist of them saying I do.

Wait a fucking a minute. Simone shouted out, are you fucking delusional? Judge you should arrest her for breaking and entering, destroying of property and just for being a nosey fat jealous bitch.

ENOUGH! The judge stopped Mona's story and had her escorted out of the room. The look on Viola's face was fiery as she watched Mona walk out the door.

The judge charged us both for assault and breaking and entering. Our bail was set to fifty thousand a piece thanks to my bomb ass lawyer. Of course, I had my bail money but still had to do six months. Simone didn't have the funds to free herself, and neither did I. Hell, I already had to pay for her lawyer and another thousand for him to fly all the way to Springfield. It was over for her. I told her I was going to make sure she was okay in there for taking the blame for initiating the assault. But only so I can get home and start my operation back up. The judge gave her twenty-four months flat. Two years didn't seem so bad. My dad always said if you do the crime you got to do the time that's only if you get caught. I couldn't stomach to look at him after watching those clips of me. I was too ashamed. I didn't know that incident was going to backfire on us so soon though. My mom was still in disbelief her little girl wasn't so innocent and couldn't believe I was charged with breaking and entering, especially after my uncle, her brother got murdered when I was eleven years old for the same thing. Something about a neighbor having twenty pounds of marijuana in his basement and he just had to take it. An old man had shot him straight in the back with a riffle used to hunt deer. I made sure we were discreet, which reminded me to reach out to Mona about it. Until, I realized god is good I could've been in there doing two years with Simone so let me just stop acting like I just did crazy time. I didn't know this lifestyle was going to come with a lot of physical problems. The only thing on my mind once I got back home was making money. I could've sat and dwelled on the situation and the shadiness of my friends but it was behind me. I no longer cared, and couldn't anything or no-one else take anything away from me at this point.

CHAPTER 11

Viola had no friends, man, or customers. Her reputation had hit rock bottom. She only been living in Springfield for a year now and had already been considered a hoe to everyone. She had to start over from scratch, you would've thought she learned her lesson from that six-month bid which felt like forever. Viola had beat up her friend for something she thought she did. Even though she was contemplating on sabotaging her as well, she still felt wrong. At the end of the day she was still going to be punished behind her actions she just didn't think it was going to be that drastic. All the facts she thought she had on everyone was wrong. She couldn't believe it was Mona this whole time. I sat and did jail time with a bunch of gay pussy licking dykes, all because I let a lame in my circle. Viola thought she should stay behind the scenes this go round. She thought to gather up a few girls around her age that seemed very shy and innocent and transform them into who she was. Viola knew she had to get her mojo back and her clientele up Immediately. The only thing she had to her name was her place and car. Money had gotten tight, she had to sell all her belong-ings to start over. Well at least pay for the girls she had in mind a makeover.

The next day a man knocked on her door with a package. It was her neighbor, he said it had been sitting there for months. Viola thanked him and shut the door. Not again Viola said.

As she ripped the box apart. It was a picture frame of her and Trey that said just married. It was a wedding gift he wanted to place at their new crib he was surprising her with. He wrote her a letter

"To the love of my life, I can no longer Imagine life without you. I can no longer sleep without you near me. I bought this house for us to remind you how much I love and adore you. As long as you're by my side you will never have to worry about anything. I put my right hand up to god, every stress worry or concerns you have consider them over with at this very moment. You are my biggest cheerleader, you love me so good. Our sex is beyond passionate, and I just love the way you smile. I'm giving you my last name and hopefully you have my child. Put this picture next to your bed, and think of me every time."

'FIANCE

My heart was warm as a tear fell from my eye. The good life I always Imagined in college was over in a blink of an eye. I never really thought my life would flip that quickly, it happened so fast. I remember running through the airport about to miss my flight. Who would've known I'd be in this position nine months after. It's funny how life works, viola said as she placed the picture back in the box. For some reason, I don't know why I keep dwelling over it. Something still felt out of place. I just didn't have it in me to figure it out. Slipping on an old pair of Gucci sandals, there wasn't a way I was getting rid of these. Viola laughed to herself. The garage sell was tomorrow and I had everything I didn't want any more boxed up. Well I wanted all my shit, but the way my bank account was set up I could've sold my damn arm if I had to. I wasn't used to being so broke. I always vision being in a position to be on top and stay on top. Even though bosses take losses, I never was with the cliché myth. I never wanted to take a lost! Once I was able to actually make it out and win, I was going to make sure I stayed winning at all cost. Even if it costed me my life. That attitude was the reason I just did six months in jail. My mom always hated my smart mouth. I was just too determine to become famous or some shit. My dad, even though he's mad at me right now, I know I'm still his little princess and he wants nothing but the best for me. I'm twenty-three years old with the mindset of a thirty-year-old. Wait, let me not rush it, I don't want to be that old. I can picture me now bitter with a few cats because men of that age want to be in control and doesn't anyone run me. Viola kissed her black patent leather Chanel for the last time, placing it into the other box.

The next day as I sat at the park, arranging all my goods and services. I poured me a glass of red wine to have the strength to deal with the strangers and these nappy headed kids that was running around. I even had to chase a snotty nose little girl through the water sprinklers for running off with my Cartier bracelets thinking they were mini Frisbees. A group of girls approached my stand with a stun looked. They were all so amazed at what they were seeing. One girl said, "Did we just walk into luxury park" grabbing my alexander McQueen bag modeling it back and forth. They were every bit of nine-teen. I'm guessing they were thinking my bags were knock offs the way they were waving their little twenties and tens up in the air. I laughed knowing if me and Simone seen some shit like this how we would've reacted. Knowing Simone ass, she would've plotted on snatching them all and running. Even though I wasn't that much older than them I still wasn't going to spare them or the twenty dollar bill the little girl with the blue hair kept trying to give me.

I had to break it to them nicely, there wasn't no way they could afford these. Hearing as though they didn't have a job and how they were spending their allowance. I wanted to insight them on how to work for the things they wanted. I'm not your parents and trust I don't want to be, but take this advice and run with it as I stood up on a folded picnic chair holding a tree for balance. You can be anything in this world, don't ever let anyone tell you anything differently. Its four of you and the way you all laugh, play and hang I take it as you are all best friends. Stay true to one another you will never know where it may get you. Loyalty goes along way. By the time, you are my age you can possibly have all these things. One girl raised her eyebrow looking at me as if she knew I was either their age or a few years older. But that didn't matter, at nine-teen I was into all kind of shit. Wasn't no way in hell I could afford bags and Gucci heels. I didn't even know they existed. I was trying to put them in a better mindset. Everything made sense to me. In plus, it's better than hearing your parents preach to you all day about chores and how they weren't getting the new Jordan's every week. I was trying to put them on game by teaching them the game. Hell, why not the way their shirts was tied up showing off their belly rings and how the crease in their denim shorts showed their coochie print they seemed hot and ready to me. The blue headed loud girl had to be the leader out the pack and the more advanced one. She had her uniform clothes balled up in a plastic bag as if she changed soon as the bell rung. Hot little whore, something my mom would have said.

As I preached to them for a few minutes making sure we were all on the same page. We made up a loyalty hand shake. So you mean to tell us don't graduate and go to college? And my name is Asia by the way, You keep calling me blue hair, and it was starting to get on my nerves. She smartly said as the other girls laughed at her comment interrupting my last words. I starred at her with an intriguing look knowing I couldn't get mad, her attitude was sassy just like mine. After learning their names, I proceeded on with my teaching. I know you girls are ready now. Right? Viola said staring each of them directly in the eye. Remember this game come with a lot of fun and confusion, it's only confusing if you act confused. But we shouldn't have any confusion because you all are very Loyal, right? Swear to never to tell a soul? Viola raised her left hand to get them to see she was serious. We promise Big sis, the girls all said in unison. I never told them my name. I told them to acknowledge me as big sis at all time. I gave them all each a free handbag to feel somewhat Important and took them back to my condominium to give them the talk I first gave Simone when she started.

It was a fun Thursday night. I let the girls sleep over my house. I told them to skip school Friday because we had a lot to accomplish tomorrow. We were getting to it right away. That whole night I spent showing them the ropes and how to talk to men. I had to drop Asia off at school for an hour and go get her right afterwards because her mom calls her first hour math teacher every day to make sure she had received extra credit. Her mom wanted her to get into Florida law school so bad. Only if her mom knew her daughter was as hot as a rock. The only place she was getting accepted into was Cheetahs gentlemen club or Violas get rich operation. Out of all the girls in her clique, her parents were most strict. Seeing why she was so damn fast and advanced. Her parents didn't let her do much of anything. Luckily, I had still had my hair bin and makeup kit to style them up a little. This 1998 pin up they all had going on was driving me crazy. These girls had the potential to run the company and recruit more girls of their kind. But I didn't want them to get beside themselves and forget the main mission. The money! They weren't that smart anyway. They would've went back to school with designer bags and new hairstyles, the other kids would've wondered what they were up too. I didn't want to take that chance. If anything, I wanted Asia to be the one to keep it running, after she took that tacky blue hair out of her head that is. She was more like me and was head strong. A few weeks later we were on to something and the girls were making money. I made sure they paid me first and I gave them back what I wanted them to have. I didn't want to play them, even though they really didn't care. To have all these different labels on going to school was enough for them. To know they wasn't virgins was even more better, so I explained to them that the power was in the vagina. They could charge whatever they felt their pussy deserved. I didn't want to be seen with them or even on the scene for that matter. Everywhere I went people stared, I guess they recognized my face all over the news. You would've thought I killed someone the way they reacted when they seem me in the stores. My reputation at that this point was fucked. Every time I thought about it I wanted to go kill Mona. I haven't even see her fat ass around anywhere. I'm thinking she skipped town. Knowing her, she was probably still try-ing to stalk my life. They had put a restraining order out on me, I couldn't be nowhere near forty feet of her. So dramatic! Right?

That evening I had a surprise for the girls. I told them to meet me at the park dressed up with the clothes I have given them. I wanted to take them to a lowkey night club where all the drug dealers hung out at. I knew the men in there would love to see new faces, young at that. The way their bodies was laying it was easy to bag one of them horny knuckle head niggas. Asia was on top of her game, she started walking around with her head up like she was untouchable, unshakeable, and unfuckwitable. She walked like her pussy could never stank. She carried new bags she had pur-chased with her own few dollars while all the other girls carried the same bag I had given them. I told her to be careful with how she flossed around, all that confidence creates envy. It'll create hatred and jealously from your own friends. It was just in a woman's nature to hate on the next when they can't compare. It had nothing to do with her at all, that's just the reality of being that bitch. And so that's what happened, her friend India started to do her own thing, she was another Simone. She wanted exactly what I had. I had seen India look at Asia with that same envied stare. I laughed, because I know all about it, I been there I experienced those types of friend-ships. So, I told Asia to be careful, and since she ran her circle to kick her out of the group. People like that always confuses the main mission. In which, I told them to never forget. The minute you get the mission confused with personal issues is when your whole shit fail. We needed none of that around us. I couldn't afford to take another loss. India had to go and Asia had to tell her. Nothing personal just business. Asia was a boss at this point in her own mind and I never wanted to make her feel less than that. However, she had to make that change and make it asap. Asia didn't quite have the balls to tell her because it was one of her best friends, she just didn't believe the game I was kicking to her about India. She swore India was nothing like that. I been in your shoes before, I was so naïve until, a bitch ruined my life. A bitch like India. She wanted to have everything I had, she even wanted to fuck my nigga. I used to think my mom was tripping, but your mom knows whose right and wrong for you the minute she sees it. Moms tells no lie.

As my little sister, I need you to focus, pay attention to what I'm saying. I'm not going to stir you wrong, you're winning now. You got enough to drop any kind of whip you want at nineteen. None of them girls are laying like you. Everyone will start to wonder how you're getting money, your mom will ask you a million questions then start to investigate. And guess who will be the one to spread that information on the low. India! You know why? Because she doesn't really want you to have what you have and It's too late she's already jealous. So even if she does her own thing. Her only mission and goal would be to shit on you. She's going to ruin herself quicker than anything and anybody because her intentions are wrong. You can do and befriend whoever you want. But when you are under me, you gone do what I tell you to do. Asia starred at me with a confused face. She was so lost; baby girl didn't have a clue to what I was saying.

Listen when you get to a certain level in your life. You must separate your-self from the rest. You have to change the way you think, and the way you move. You want to be just like me, right? Yes I do, Asia responded nervously.

Well get on it. Make me happy today! Viola responded back as she grinned and walked away.

How am I going to tell India I can't be her friend anymore? Asia sat and played with her fingers for a while. Even though Viola made a little sense in some way, she knew her friend India was nothing like that.

The next day in school, India ran up to Asia. Hey girl guess what? What! Asia responded in a nonchalant tone. Chris asked me to go to the movies with him tonight, you know how long I've been waiting on this day. Should I go? India asked.

If you want, slamming her locker.

Are you on your period or something, why you seeming so aggy today? India flipped Asia hair.

I'm good girl, I just... Never mind grabbing a strapless tank top from out her bag.

Well should I go, you still haven't answered the question. I said yes girl if you want.

Rolling her eyes uncontrollably. You've been acting different lately. India said

That new Celine bag got you feeling yourself.

What do my bag have to do with me feeling myself it's only a purse, But if I wanted to feel myself I can shit I paid for it. Asia reminded India as she walked out the exit doors.

Later that evening Asia linked back up with Viola. She told her she told India that she couldn't be down and made up a short story on how she reacted.

That's my girl, Viola smiled. Now it's time we take it up a few notches.

What's a few notches, what are we going to do now.

You ask too many questions little sis, just follow my lead I would never stir you wrong.

Viola took Asia to the Hawks basketball game. They had to blend well in the stands so no one could recognize them. Well Viola for that matter. I'm going to show you how to get a few ball players. You see, this is a different type of money. These dudes are committed with signed contracts. Which mean their money is guaranteed, it'll never run out. Since you're a newbie you have to start finessing, I started a little bit different I had no help and no one telling me what to do. I'm going to elevate you and install the proper knowledge into you so you will never want or need for any-thing another day in your life. Soon, you will be the flyest nine-teen year old in Springfield. Viola jokingly said, rubbing her fingers through her hair.

What would my mom say, seeing me with all this shit? Viola laughed, honey you are grown. You can do whatever you want to. Shit move out, you don't have to worry about her rules anymore. You are making your own money, you can probably take care of her.

Now listen to me, I'm going to show you how you pleasantly walk pass security. Don't walk pass as if your sneaking, making it obvious that you're a groupie or fan. Walk through like you supposed to be back there. Head to the lady's room, fix your hair a little and spray on some jimmy choo. When you see them in the locker room which is directly across from the bathroom. Walk out!

Viola had Asia looking like American's next top model. She stared at her amused and fascinated tilting her head checking her teeth for red smears from her lipstick. Asia was the bomb, and her body type wasn't the typical teenager body type. She pretty much had it in the bag with finessing men. Her charm and attitude was enough to get them and keep them wrapped around her finger. To top her off her booty was fat, with tiny boobs and a small waist to match.

I'm going to text your phone when I see them exiting the court. Make sure you are alert and aware of what's going on. Viola gave Asia a comprehensive nod to keep them on the same page. Moments later, Asia came walking out the lady's room. Her eyes widen as if she had seen Jesus himself. Tall, muscular, and sweaty men was running towards her, she didn't know rather to run or faint. The way Viola was about her money, she knew she couldn't fuck this up.

Hey, are you looking for something slim. A man approached her breathing hard as ever as Asia went into a quick daze,. Stuttering trying to respond back. Are you lost? He said lifting her chin up to catch eye contact. Asia smiled as she quickly snapped out of her daydream. Yes, I am, actually. I was looking for the women's restroom. It's right behind you miss.

Asia turned around so hesitant and nervous. Thinking what would Viola say know-ing she had an opportunity but fucked it up. He reached for her arm as she walked away and asked her name. She was so thrown off at how white and straight his teeth were that she forgot the question. Excuse me, she asked. Your name, I said what's your name? he replied. Is everything okay?

Yes, everything is cool. Getting herself together. My name is Asia. I'm sorry I never been to a game before so all day I've been extremely excited. No apologizes, my name is Trey.

Nice to meet you, trey. Do you work for the arena, or you're just hanging around waiting on pictures and autographs? Trey laughed. You are very hilarious. I'm not waiting on no damn picture, I am the picture. I'm the star player. You might be roaming around waiting to take a picture with me. Trey babbled.

Asia went into a swift stun, already imagining having sex with him in her head. He was so fine, her vagina soaked immediately. and at that point she didn't care if he paid her or not. She knew she was either about to change his life or he was about to change hers. They exchanged numbers and gave one last quick glance, I'll see you soon. Trey muttered as they both walked away....

CHAPTER 12

Did you have fun yesterday? Viola peeked over to ask Asia. I did. Asia responded. Well, do you have anything for me. I know what that glow mean, you bagged a basketball player, didn't you? Only men of ball status can make you glow like that. Pushing Asia with a light giggle, waiting on her to spill the beans. There's nothing to tell, I met a few dudes around the way that I'll be meeting with them tomorrow night. I got to try an make time for them all, my mom wants me to go visit my aunt with her Saturday morning. Viola didn't want to control her much, she just wanted HER MONEY. All the time she invested into her, she didn't have any more play in her. I'll pay you whatever I make when I get back Sunday morning. Okay, make sure you on your shit. I'm going to try and get out here myself to see what I can do. Viola said.

Speaking of what you can do. Why don't I ever see you doing anything. Asia won-dered aloud. Asia was getting a little bit too beside herself, but I had to remember I needed her, I couldn't cut too deep into her so I kicked it to her politely. I'm a very discreet business woman. You or anyone else will never know when or how I move. I told you I learned my lesson with that before. I do everything on my time. Not your time, not uncles Sam time. I run shit around here you got that! Viola smartly re-sponded. Asia was so caught up in whatever her and someone was texting she wasn't even paying full attention to what I was saying. Little whore.

I'll call you Sunday when I get back. Grabbing her belongings switching out the door. Later that night, Viola was craving her favorite dish, chicken jumbo soup with Italian cheese bread. It seems like ever since her incident she was afraid to be seen, She knew being the Ex fiancé of trey would bring so much noise and attention her way. Even though, it wasn't that deep. She just couldn't fathom the attention any-more. Viola finally chucked the pressure up of going out and having a good time. She got glammed up, threw on some heels and a dress and took the night out on the town. There wasn't no way she was going to let some people who never mattered stop her whole life. As she jumped into her car. She sat in the parking lot getting the urge to be that bitch again. She didn't know if it was the late night old-school mix they was playing on the radio, or if she was just feeling herself again.

I swear doing a six-month bid would make you look at life a whole lot different. But face it, I was locked in. Viola talked to herself for a while, navigating Olives soup kitchen into her gps.

Pulling up to the restaurant in mid-town. She forgot how lavish that side of town was. I mean, she lived in a nice neighborhood but mid-town was were it all started. I remember making my first couple thousands in this parking lot. Viola stepped out of her car, fixing her strap and pulling down her dress. She alarmed her car twice to make sure it was completely locked. She looked around to make sure no one would recognize her and walked in the restaurant.

Hello, Mrs. Fergurson where would you like to be seated today. Viola heart pumped thinking he was either trying to be funny or just didn't know what was going on. She politely grabbed the menu and walked to her booth.

Sipping on an olive cocktail, a man kindly approach her. Hey, is anyone sitting here? Viola looked up with an impressed grin. Seeing how tailored and cut his suit was, Thinking, rather or not she should lie. She really wanted to sit alone, But the thought of his potential conversation allowed her to let him sit down. Sooner than later the conversation started to heat up and viola was one more drink from being under the influence. As they both laughed about absolutely nothing. I guess they were both in need of a drink or two. Excusing himself to go to the gentlemen's room. Viola laughed to herself, asking the bartender for the bill.

Viola sat and ate while she waited on the guy to return. She didn't catch his name or contact, she just knew he was from Vegas but here on business. Any business conversation was enough for her to chat about anything. While realizing twenty minutes had went by and he still wasn't back. She figured he had left so she paid for her food and searched for the bathroom. Walking into the restroom, all the stalls were being used. So, she checked herself out in the mirror until one was vacant. Leaving the restroom and searching for her car key she had realized she left them on the bath-room sink. Are you looking for these, a deep voice asked. Viola looked up, it was the clean suit guy that left her at the bar.

How did you get these? Viola said with an awkward stare. I seen when you placed them down. How, did you see me? Huh? What? Viola was confused. I didn't know that was the guys room. I could've sworn I seen a dress on the door. No, you're not hallucinating. You were in the right room, I was waiting on you. Viola took a step back, waiting on me for what? The guy leaned in closer, waiting on you to come take care of me. Viola faced squinched up, trying to figure out what it was he was hinting at. I wanted you to fuck me like you never fuck anyone else in your life. Winking his eye, Viola went into a daze trying to stop her rage from slapping the shit out of him. Seconds later she snatched her keys from the grip of his hand and ran out the door. The guy chased after her, aren't you a prostitute, He said in an outrageous scream. Isn't this what you do, I seen you all over the news? Viola stopped running knowing at that moment wasn't no way the streets would ever respect her again. She took her hair from out her ponytail, letting it blow through the wind, turned around to eye him down slowly. As she walked closer, she fixed his collar, straightened out his tie, whispered in his ear and said, "My prices just went back up, and if you want me to FUCK YOU like that you whack piece of shit, you have to catch me in Vegas, where selling pussy is legal!"

THE END

To be continued…..

Printed in the United States
By Bookmasters